Archdeac

Also by C A Alington

Archdeacons Ashore
Blackmail in Blankshire
Gold and Gaiters

ARCHDEACONS AFLOAT

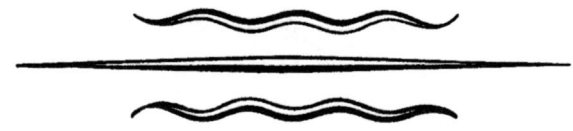

C. A. ALINGTON

Ostara Publishing

First published in 1946
by Faber and Faber Limited

Every reasonable effort has been made by the Publisher to establish whether any person or institution holds the copyright for this work. The Publisher invites any persons or institutions that believe themselves to be in possession of any such copyright to contact them at the address below.

ISBN 978-1-906288-06-8

A CIP reference is available from the British Library

Printed and Bound in the United Kingdom

Published by	Ostara Publishing
13 King Coel Road
Lexden
Colchester
CO3 9AG

THIS IS DONE
FOR THE DIVERSION
OF OUR THOUGHTS

THE PRIEST

IN

Don Quixote

CHAPTER XXXII

TO DAVID AND JONATHAN

Contents

I.	TWO MEN IN A BOAT	*page* 9
II.	THE FIRST SHOCK	16
III.	THE SECOND SHOCK	23
IV.	THE THIRD SHOCK	30
V.	A DAY IN CRETE	35
VI.	SIDELIGHTS ON POLITICS	45
VII.	SLEUTHS IN ATHENS	52
VIII.	DISAPPEARANCE IN DELOS	60
IX.	THE ARCHDEACON AT BAY	66
X.	GAMES AT OLYMPIA	75
XI.	THE JOURNEY	83
XII.	AN ANXIOUS INTERLUDE	92
XIII.	THE BRIGAND CHIEF	97
XIV.	THE LETTER	110
XV.	PREPARATIONS	123
XVI.	MICHALIS	127
XVII.	THE GREAT ASSAULT	134
XVIII.	LADY MARY'S DILEMMA	140
	EPILOGUE	147

CHAPTER I

Two Men in a Boat

"As idle as a painted ship
Upon a painted Ocean."
—Coleridge

The Archdeacon of Thorp, the Ven. John Craggs, was lying in a chair on deck, engaged in an animated conversation with his brother Archdeacon, the Ven. James Castleton of Garminster. This was in itself a surprising fact, for archdeacons, as a class, are not gregarious. There is among them none of that impressive solidarity which causes bishops of the most diverse views to seek one another's company at constant meetings, and brings even deans occasionally together for brief and acrimonious conference. Archdeacons are a lonely body, conscious, it is to be feared, of that ill-name which so long was theirs. There is no medieval jest so frequently recalled, and none which raised so sure a laugh among our ancestors, as the inquiry "whether an archdeacon can be saved", and the irony would seem to have entered into their innocent souls. To see two archdeacons conversing together was indeed something of a portent.

That it was not so regarded by the other passengers on the S.S. *Lucretia*, chartered by the Hellenic Travellers' Club for a pleasure cruise in the Mediterranean, was due to the fact that neither was wearing archidiaconal costume or was printed as "Venerable" on the passenger list. The former circumstance was due to their common feeling that gaiters and gaiety went ill together; the latter calls for slightly fuller explanation. Archdeacon

Two Men in a Boat

Craggs, the younger and less conventional of the two, frankly preferred to take his holidays as an apparent layman: in the case of the Archdeacon of Garminster, the ship's printer had made an error, so that he figured as the Rev. James Castleton.

Though they shared a cabin, it was not for a day or two that they themselves discovered their common dignity. The Archdeacon of Thorp, an execrable sailor, was prostrated with seasickness immediately on leaving Plymouth: some acid remarks which, apparently in delirium, he let fall about the Ecclesiastical Commissioners, had suggested to his companion that they had interests in common, and, the Bay of Biscay once passed, their acquaintance had ripened into friendship. Craggs was young, tall, passably good-looking and decided in his utterance: Castleton elderly, plain, and benevolent: the Archdeacon of Thorp, though his dignity was but of two years' standing, was already beginning to be a name of terror to negligent clergy under his supervision, while the Bishop of Garminster had been heard to lament, with an affectionate sigh, that in his archdeacon's ministrations the velvet glove was more apparent than the iron hand. But they shared an unregenerate passion for the game of bridge, and the distinction which they drew between it and such games as poker was as convinced—and perhaps as illogical—as that which some temperance enthusiasts have been known to draw between cider and other alcoholic drinks. Even an unfortunate episode in the Gulf of Lions, when Craggs, having bid an impossible contract, had been forced by seasickness to withdraw at the precise moment when it became demonstrably unmakeable, had not brought about any rupture in their relations.

It was, in fact, of bridge, and not (as might have been expected) of dilapidations, or of the delinquencies of the inferior clergy, that they were talking at the moment.

They agreed in lamenting the tendency to introduce complications from across the Atlantic, which gave Craggs the opportunity of recalling Lord Dunraven's acid remark that "yacht racing in America demanded too close an attention to business to be consistent with an Englishman's idea of sport."

"I like Americans very much," he remarked, "but there's no denying they are distressingly competent, and take everything much too seriously! I suppose it comes of being so young: one gets more tolerant, or perhaps lazier, as one gets older. Certainly on a holiday one doesn't want to be worried with something uncommonly like the higher mathematics."

"Yes, this is a good type of holiday," agreed his companion, stretching his legs lazily. "Of course, these Hellenic tours provide some very intelligent lectures, but I confess to being rather glad that attendance is not compulsory."

"The great thing about Hellenic tours", observed Craggs sententiously, "is that you can be reasonably sure that your fellow-passengers won't either wear too little or drink too much—and that's a comfort in these days!"

They lay in silence for a time, watching their more energetic companions dutifully parading the deck. As Craggs had been confined to his cabin for several days, he had not had much opportunity of making the acquaintance of his fellow-travellers, so that Castleton had to act for the most part as showman. "Poor old Tomkins!" he remarked, as the ship's official lecturer passed by, obviously explaining some classical point to a young lady with a craving for information. "I am told he has never been the same man since a day when the ship passed Stromboli one evening in the middle of one of his discourses: it was in eruption, and all his audience slipped silently away in the dark to the Stromboli side, while he held forth on the other. Of course, it is a regular clerical nightmare to dream that one's congregation vanishes in the middle of one's sermon, but it was bad luck for him to have to compete with a real live volcano!"

"But surely Tomkins isn't the lecturer I remember on one of these cruises a few years ago?"

"No, he is a kind of understudy, who comes when the real man is not available; he is a delightful old fellow, and very learned, but somehow I don't think he has quite got the feel of the *Lucretia* in the way the other man had after years of practice: at least that is what I gather."

"What a comfort it is to feel that one knows nobody on board," said Craggs, "or rather that nobody knows one in one's normal existence! There's nothing like that to give one the real holiday feeling!"

"Ye-es," agreed the Archdeacon of Garminster, a little doubtfully. "But I have a horrid feeling that there is a lady on board who knows who I am. I have not the least idea who she is, but then I am so shortsighted that I am always getting into trouble for failing to recognize people I really know quite well—but she gave me a nasty look when she went by just now, as if she knew me and thought I ought to know her. There she comes again!" The Archdeacon hurriedly raised a paper, and studied it earnestly until the danger was over.

"She certainly looked this way," said his colleague, when she had gone by: "middle-aged, grey-haired, spectacled—does that suggest anything to you?"

"My dear Craggs," said Castleton with a sigh. "You must realize that Garminster swarms with virtuous ladies of that description! No, all I can do is to be as careful as I can."

"Why not try a red tie?" asked the Archdeacon of Thorp. "I find that helps the disguise quite a lot."

"Ah, but the worst of it is", said his friend, with a sigh, "I am down as a parson in the passenger list, and some of them would be sure to be shocked if I went into colours! Now you are safe, so far as that goes. There is nothing I can do except to hope for the best."

"Do you remember the story Bishop Paget used to tell about the optimist who fell down the liftshaft at the Hotel Cecil? 'Even then' (he used to say), 'the poor fellow's constitutional optimism did not desert him: for, as he passed each landing, he was heard to call out in loud and cheerful tones: "All right—so far!" ' I feel a bit like that myself, though not quite so hopeful. You see, for one thing, I've not been much in the public eye so far, with this foul seasickness, so that I haven't had a fair test up to date, and, for another, there are all those people who got on at Toulon, who've hardly shown up yet: there may be all sorts of dangers for us both among them—still, one can always hope!"

They resumed their peaceful contemplation of the passers-by.

"That's a nice-looking girl," observed Craggs as a young lady in the early twenties passed. "Do you happen to know who she is?"

"Yes, she is a Miss Hillcroft—at least I think that is the name—she has come as companion to old Lady Mary Culham, and I am afraid she finds her rather a handful."

"Who's Lady Mary?" asked Craggs.

"I forget who she is exactly, but there is no excuse for anyone not knowing she has a nephew who's a Duke—she is always dragging him into the conversation. I do not want to be uncharitable, but I am much afraid she is one of those selfish old creatures who think they were made to be waited on, and everyone else made to wait on them—and the result is that poor Miss Hillcroft hardly ever gets a moment to herself. I have seen very little of her myself, but everyone seems to like her. I wonder", he went on meditatively, "why old ladies are always either so very nice or so very unpleasant!"

"It is funny what queer people seem to come on these trips," he added after a while. "Look at that stout lady with all the pearls!

One would not have thought that Greek antiquities would make much appeal to her. I do not know her name, but I believe she is the widow of a big business man in Manchester, multiple shops of some kind, I fancy."

"A good many of her younger sisters don't look as if classical learning would be their strong suit," observed Craggs, " but the female sex is amazingly persistent, and I suppose quite a lot of them hope that old Tomkins will turn them into ripe scholars before the cruise is over!"

"'The desire of the moth for the star,'" murmured his brother archdeacon, who had a liking for the more familiar type of great poetry, and enjoyed quoting it.

"Anyhow they won't singe their wings in the process! You know I have a theory that it's just intentional suicide which drives moths into candle-flames. Fancy having to live on rugs and old clothes! I'm sure I should take the short way out myself if I was one of them. But that's a curious couple that went by just now," he went on, "a fellow who looks like a Greek, with an ugly Englishman in tow."

"Yes, he is a Greek, called Michalis, and the Englishman's name is Blades. I saw them playing at deck-tennis the other day and happened to hear their names."

"Blades doesn't look as if lectures were much in his line!"

"No, but I daresay he will get as much out of them as poor old Lady Mary: she sat fast asleep all through one of them last night, in the front row: it must have been a little disconcerting for Tomkins."

"And what about those schoolboys?" went on Craggs. "But they'll certainly get some fun out of the cruise one way or another. There's a stern-looking woman going by now: do you know who she is? You're a regular encyclopædia!"

"Yes, she is a Miss Bustard from Cambridge, a very learned lady: I am told she is a great classical scholar. I fancy", went on

Castleton, who was not above an interest in gossip, "I fancy she is something of a thorn in the side of poor Tomkins, for she is always on the look out to catch him in some blunder, and, learned as he is, he is by no means above making a slip now and then. Much of the criticism I am speaking of appears to be inspired by her. I am afraid that there is a trace of snobbishness in the matter, for Tomkins, though no doubt an excellent fellow, does not come from either of the older universities."

"Miss Bustard should be reminded", said Craggs, "that there must have been a time in the Middle Ages when Cambridge itself was regarded as a mushroom provincial affair! I don't care where Tomkins comes from, provided he can lecture—but I'd gathered from you that he was something of a windbag."

"Surely, surely not!" protested his friend, much distressed. "I am sure I never said..."

"Oh no, you never said so. As far as I remember, what you said was that he was 'in some danger of being carried away by the interest of his subject', and I thought that was your charitable way of putting it. I'll go and listen myself next time. But if I'm going to be lectured to, I must have some sleep first!"

To others of the *Lucretia*'s passengers, the reader will be introduced in due course: for the rest it may be said that the Captain was, when things went well, a genial figure, presiding at his table with much acceptance, but with a capacity for forcible expression, if things went amiss, which maintained the high traditions of the Service—and, if the truth must be told, with a somewhat tepid appreciation both of classical antiquities in themselves and of the tourists who thronged to admire them: and that the junior officers were as charming, and the stewards and stewardesses as attentive as every passenger on the *Lucretia* had long learnt to expect.

CHAPTER II

The First Shock

"Lend me your ears."
—SHAKESPEARE

It must not be supposed that our two friends, in their desire to avoid recognition, had lived the lives of archidiaconal hermits. On the contrary, their table in the dining saloon was the meeting-place of a cheerful company. Its other most lively members were a Mr. and Mrs. Wilson, a young married couple from Herefordshire, while a more sober element was supplied by Mr. Birtley, a housemaster at the well-known school of Harchester, who concealed beneath a somewhat pompous manner a keen sense of humour, and whose love for clothing his opinions in stately polysyllables gave much entertainment to the rest.

The sixth and last member of the party was a somewhat taciturn Yorkshireman, named Pycroft, whose precise occupation was obscure, but who listened with apparent appreciation to the conversation of the rest. He played a very good game of bridge, and as the Wilsons did not play, the others formed a regular quartette. The archdeacons, it need not be said, anxious to discourage inquiry into their own antecedents, made no researches into his, and gratefully accepted his godly monitions at the bridge table. Mr. Craggs was accepted as a leisured layman with the scholarly interests appropriate to a member of the Hellenic Travellers' Club, while Castleton was regarded as a country parson.

The First Shock

If we listen for a few minutes to their conversation, we shall form some opinion of their characters.

"Wasn't it a pity that Stromboli was doing none of his tricks as we passed!" said Mrs. Wilson, whose conversation was of the nature commonly described as "bright".

"I'm told on reliable authority", said Mr. Craggs, "that Dr. Tomkins was seen surreptitiously shaking his fist at it as we went by: it looks as if the old grievance was still rankling!"

"What's his grievance?" asked Mr. Pycroft.

Mr. Castleton explained.

"The pyrotechnical effects of Nature inevitably put mere oratorical fireworks into the shade," observed Mr. Birtley.

"I was so glad to see Sicily," went on Mrs. Wilson. "What a lovely island it looks!"

"The oranges looked pretty good to me," remarked her husband.

" 'Golden lamps in a green night,' " murmured the Archdeacon of Garminster.

"The word 'orange'," observed Mr. Birtley, "has had a somewhat remarkable history. It is a curious freak of fortune that the name of a small town on the Rhone has become he watchword of Protestant fanaticism in a remote Northern island."

"My grandparents came from Ulster," remarked Mr. Pycroft to no one in particular.

"But what's that got to do with oranges?" interposed Mr. Wilson in the interests of peace. "Do you know that, Mr. Birtley?"

"Nothing, I fancy," replied he. "I understand that the name of the fruit is Arabic in origin: the Arabs, as of course you know, held Sicily for quite a long time."

"I hope you noticed Charybdis as we went through the Straits, Mrs. Wilson?" said the Archdeacon of Garminster.

"Oh yes, but I was *dreadfully* disappointed! It looked such a very tame little affair; I was hoping for a real whirlpool.

The First Shock

I can't see what old Ulysses—it was Ulysses wasn't it?—made all that fuss about it for!"

"He was in a jolly small boat, Mary," said her husband. "It's all very well for you in a boat of 30,000 tons."

"Less," remarked Mr. Pycroft.

"Well, anyhow, a pretty big boat—it's all very well for you to laugh at it, but I can quite imagine a rowboat getting into baddish trouble—besides, it may have been a lot bigger in his day."

"The ultimate hope of all sufferers from seasickness", observed Mr. Birtley, "lies in the creation of a vessel large enough to reduce the convulsions of the Atlantic to the dimensions of the ripples on a millpond: that is the direction in which the construction of our great luxury liners unmistakeably points."

"What a ghastly thought!" said Craggs, laughing. "Shocking sailor as I am, I devoutly hope I shan't live to see that!"

"Like a Channel tunnel?" asked Pycroft.

"I trust Mr. Craggs will never allow his patriotism to yield to paltry considerations of personal convenience," said Mr. Birtley.

"Well, anyhow, I'm very glad I didn't live in those old days," said Mrs. Wilson. "The Gulf of Lions was a good deal too much for me even in a great boat like this!"

"You certainly made fuss enough about it," remarked her husband. "I don't like to think how you'd have got on in the Ark if you'd been married to Shem or Ham, or any of those chaps!"

"The complaints of the beasts in the Ark," said Mr. Pycroft, unexpectedly.

"Would necessitate further remark,
If they had not been voiced
In When it was Moist,
By the author of When it was Dark!"

"I'm glad you like the Limerick metre, Mr. Pycroft," said the Archdeacon of Thorp: "as we are reasonably near Tarentum, you must allow me to quote one which Bishop Gore used to recite with great pleasure:

> *There was an old man of Tarentum,*
> *Who gnashed his false teeth till he bent 'em;*
> *When asked what it cost*
> *To replace them when lost,*
> *He replied "Well, I can't tell—I rent 'em!"* '

"How grand Etna looks!" said Mrs. Wilson romantically, when the chuckles had died away. "I'm so looking forward to seeing it from Taormina."

"The Sicilians have good reason for calling it Mongibello, the beautiful mountain," said the Archdeacon of Garminster.

"I wish we'd seen Vesuvius," said Mrs. Wilson, "one hears such a lot about it."

"It compares very poorly with Etna," said Craggs. "I remember climbing it some years ago: the guide made a great fuss about our being careful not to fall in, which is a thing you could hardly do with all the sand there is inside the crater. The real danger is falling out into Italy, for it's quite steep on the side, and you could easily get a nasty fall."

"I confess that I have never shared the desire to immolate myself like Empedocles by plunging into the crater of Etna," remarked Mr. Birtley: "as a matter of fact, I have long cherished the suspicion that he was impelled from the rear by some of his disciples. I know several pedagogues who would need to approach the crater with considerable precaution, if any of their pupils were at hand."

"Some schoolmasters are the devil," said Mr. Pycroft, feelingly.

The visit to Taormina was duly paid, and the view of Etna behind the theatre duly admired—"Nature", as Mr. Birtley remarked, "having excelled herself as a theatrical scene painter," and it was a contented party which, in the evening, descended again to the ship.

The night had turned chilly, and Craggs, who liked a stroll on deck with a pipe before turning in, thought it wise to pick up a greatcoat. The sky had clouded over and it was a dark night into which he gazed as he leant on the rails. The decks were more or less deserted, though some of the younger members of the party were engaged in some hilarious games further aft.

He was enjoying his solitude, when he heard a quiet step approach him, and to his horror a voice which whispered urgently, "Mr. Archdeacon!"

Craggs turned sulkily, much annoyed to have been identified in spite of all his precautions; he saw a dim female figure with a scarf thrown over her head. She spoke in hurried accents.

"I'm so sorry, but there's something terrible going on! Please, will you help me?"

At that moment the noisy game players made a sudden rush in their direction, and whispering: "Please be here the same time to-morrow night—I know you'll tell me what to do"—the unknown faded into the darkness and was lost to sight.

The Archdeacon of Thorp finished his pipe in ruffled mood; he disliked mysteries of all kinds, and those involving veiled female figures were least of all to his taste. The voice had suggested nothing to him, for few of us have a whisper which can be called distinctive: he was completely puzzled, and that was another sensation both unfamiliar and distasteful to him, for he was a singularly clear-headed man. He descended to the cabin, where he found Castleton in the act of mounting his bunk.

"Look here," he said, "this is a desperate business! I don't know what to do about it"—and he recounted his adventure.

As he did so, a ray of light seemed to dawn on him.

"I tell you what!" he cried, "she must be that woman you thought had spotted you! She must have taken me for you in the dark.

The First Shock

"Yes, by Jove," he went on, gathering conviction as he spoke, "that must be it. I remember now, I picked up your greatcoat by mistake when I went on deck. Haven't you any idea who the lady can be?"

Castleton who, as we have said, was a benevolent man, was not prepared to meet so definite an assertion. He stoutly declared that he had not the least idea who the lady could be, but was unable to deny that there was some plausibility in this reconstruction of the situation, for he had been conscious of a female eye which looked at him with something like recognition. But, fortunately for him, his colleague was too generous to press his momentary advantage.

"Let's toss for it," he said. "I suppose one of us has to go and keep this abominable assignation! Why shouldn't we toss? After all, drawing lots has very distinguished biblical authority!"

Castleton gratefully agreed.

"I'll toss," said Craggs, "you haven't room to do it in that upper berth."

He spun a coin.

"Heads!" cried the Archdeacon of Garminster.

"It's tails!" said his brother archdeacon, with a sigh of relief.

Castleton passed a restless night, followed by a day which seemed as interminable as it was intolerable. Haunted by the thought that every female head might contain the eyes which had pierced his mild disguise, that every feminine dress might drape the lady he was so soon to meet, he shivered visibly at every contact with a member of the sex.

Even the dull and sleepy eyes of Lady Mary Culham seemed endowed with a penetrating power, and as for the beady optics of Mrs. Burslem, the wealthy lady of the pearls, he wilted if they so much as rested on him for a moment. Miss Bustard, too, had a piercing glance, and he felt that an eye capable of reaching to the hidden meaning of a Greek inscription would be more than capable of penetrating his disguise, if indeed trousers on an archdeacon can be held to deserve the name. He was noticeably silent and distraught at meals, and the encouragement offered him by the Archdeacon of Thorp, who now took a light-hearted view of the situation, had no power to raise his drooping spirits.

"It can't be anything very bad," he said. "You know how women love to exaggerate things. I expect she thinks someone has designs on her, and only wants a little godly counsel and advice."

Archdeacon Castleton felt singularly ill qualified to deal with such a demand: he recalled the story of the English clergyman who, when called upon to hear a confession in French, only felt able, after listening to a catalogue of lamentable misdoings, to ejaculate, "Oh, *vous avez, avez vous* ?"

Most of the afternoon he spent like a wounded animal, lurking in dark corners, and sighed more than once for the moral support which he might have derived from his gaiters. It was a jaded and jaundiced archdeacon who took his stand at the fatal hour on the appointed spot, wearing his own overcoat: the time was about an hour and a half after dinner.

He tried to divert his thoughts from the impending interview by turning them to some of the problems which he had left unsolved at home—the churchwardens who held that their vicars were little better than Papists, the vicars who thought even worse of their churchwardens; the choirs who couldn't sing at all, and the choirs who sang far more than was desirable and, above all, the masterful-looking ladies who, regarding vicars, churchwardens and organists as creatures born to do their bidding, ruled their parishes with a despotism, benevolent indeed, but wholly unconstitutional.

He tried to force himself to think of rectories too large for their occupants and of others demonstrably too small; of churches which needed building and of churches which needed pulling down; of contractors, plumbers, registrars, diocesan secretaries, and, in the last resort, of bishops. But these familiar figures had no power to grip his mind: they flitted past like phantoms, or, worse still, resolved themselves into the veiled female figure whose advent he so anxiously awaited. He would have fled, but, like Casabianca, though for very different reasons, he stood firm on the deserted deck.

The night was again dark, though lighter than the night before, and he gazed gloomily at the waters rushing by. After a delay which seemed interminable, a stealthy footstep made itself heard: again the whisper came, "Mr. Archdeacon!" The Archdeacon of Garminster turned nervously to face his doom—but, the moment that the lady saw his face revealed in the half light, she uttered a lamentable cry and fled hastily into the darkness.

CHAPTER III

The Second Shock

"Here are a few of the unpleasantest words
That ever blotted paper."
—SHAKESPEARE

The Ven. James Castleton was badly shaken. Never, since a rural dean (subsequently suspected of hydrophobia) had endeavoured to bite him in the leg, had he had so unpleasant an adventure. On that occasion his archidiaconal gaiters had stood him in good stead. But to-day he had wantonly deprived himself of such support. A ship in which strange ladies addressed unknown archdeacons by night, and fled screaming at the sight of their faces, was something entirely

The Second Shock

foreign to his experience, and promised ill for a peaceful holiday.

He made his way thoughtfully to the smoking room, where by arrangement his friend was waiting for him in a secluded corner.

"Well, what luck?" inquired he.

"It was terrible, terrible!" said the Archdeacon of Garminster, sinking into a chair in a state of exhaustion; and he narrated his adventure in detail. It was received by the Archdeacon of Thorp with undisguised merriment—so true is it that the reported sufferings of others have but little power to stir the heart!

"You certainly seem to have frightened the lady off," he said. "It reminds me of how Victor Hugo once suggested that at the Day of Judgment he would overawe the Deity 'by the majesty of his presence and the dignity of his rebuke': your presence and a mere look seem to have done the trick."

Even the gentle Castleton was somewhat nettled by his colleague's lack of sympathy, and, mild spirit as he was, he was moved to carry the war into the enemy's country.

"That is all very well," he said, "but I think it is quite clear that the lady was expecting to see *you:* she evidently wanted your advice about something, and was startled at seeing me instead. It is your affair, I am sure, whoever she may be."

This view of the situation had a sobering effect on the Archdeacon of Thorp, who, having a just and logical mind, was unable to deny that there might be some force in the argument.

"That may be so, of course," he agreed, "but, even if it is, I don't see that there's anything we can do about it. I can't go about asking all the ladies on board if they've any secrets they would like to confide to me!"

"Of course not, of course not!" said Castleton. "I should never dream of suggesting such a thing. I think, as you do, that we can only wait on events, but it is a very distressing affair, and I do not like to think what may be the end of it."

The Second Shock

"I'll deal with the lady if she turns up again," said his stout-hearted friend, and Castleton, thankful to be freed from personal responsibility, was only too glad to leave the matter there.

And there, for some time, it remained. It is true that there was one embarrassing moment. Mrs. Wilson had remarked at breakfast that it seemed a little unromantic to be peacefully consuming grape-fruit and other luxuries as they sped past the Sicilian coast.

"Ah, my dear Mrs. Wilson," said Mr. Birtley, "I see that you have not assimilated the teaching of Kipling: 'Romance', he says, 'brought up the 9.15,' and I have no doubt that the invention of grape-fruit was, in its way, a romance of horticulture. You seem to associate romance only with moonlight on dark nights and secret meetings in lonely spots."

"Well, I think Mr. Castleton must be very romantic," said the lady slily.

The Archdeacon of Garminster gave a slight shudder, which he hoped escaped observation.

"What is this accusation, Mrs. Wilson?" he asked, blushing a little in spite of himself.

"I saw you on the lonely deck last night," she said, "gazing at the sea. It's true I didn't see any lady about, but that's what I call a romantic situation!"

"I think it was only a reaction from the stuffiness of the smoking room," said Craggs, coming to the rescue. "I'm sorry to shatter Mrs. Wilson's illusions, but I'm afraid that's the truth of it!"

"Well, it *looked* romantic anyway," said Mrs. Wilson. "I thought it was so sweet of him!"

The dangerous moment passed, and, as the awaited event did not take place, life for the archdeacons on the boat resumed its accustomed round. Bridge held a first place in their thoughts during some days of smooth seafaring, and, under the expert tuition of Mr. Pycroft, both made appreciable progress. Craggs was by nature a venturesome bidder, and Castleton a timorous one, but the daring of the one and the hesitations of the other were gradually moulded into steadiness.

Mr. Birtley alone resisted the process of standardization, declaring that bridge was in danger of suffering the same fate which attended the Heroic couplet in the days of Pope, when poetry became

> *a dull mechanic art,*
> *and every warbler had his tune by heart.*

He expressed a strong preference for the "fine careless rapture" which led a player, seeing an ace and a king or two in his hand, to live dangerously and to face incalculable odds, or, to speak more exactly, odds which he had refused to calculate.

It was not till the second day after Archdeacon Castleton's adventure that any external event ruffled the even surface of their lives. On that evening a notice signed by the purser was circulated to all passengers, urging them to take all reasonable precautions with regard to any valuables which might be in their possession. No reason was given for the warning, which naturally gave rise to much vague surmise.

"It would appear", such was Mr. Birtley's sardonic comment, "that the most respectable antecedents, and even an interest in Greek archæology, do not in themselves preclude the possibility of pilfering."

"Those jewels Mrs. Burslem's always wearing are enough to make any thief's mouth water," observed Mr. Wilson. "I can't think why she doesn't hand them over to the purser."

"I can, Jack," said his wife. "What on earth would be the point of bringing them on a cruise if you couldn't ever wear them?"

"Well, there's something in that, I suppose, and she certainly does seem to get some fun out of them, so no doubt she thinks the risk's worth running."

The Second Shock

That was in fact exactly the point of view adopted by Mrs. Burslem herself: she pooh-poohed the idea of any danger, and rang the changes on her stock of jewels. Her view, which she loudly enunciated, was that the safest place for such valuables was on the person of their owner.

"Don't talk to me about safes," she would say: "the safe hasn't been invented which a clever thief can't crack. My poor dear husband was never tired of telling me to remember that: 'Emma,' he used to say, 'most safes are just a challenge to burglars'—and the very idea of our having a thief on board is just too ridiculous; don't you agree, Lady Mary?"

Lady Mary, annoyed at being disturbed, and especially at being disturbed by Mrs. Burslem, opened a sleepy eye to say that she kept her own jewels in a safe in her own cabin: that she had always done so in the past with no evil results and saw no reason to depart from her custom. Her stepmother, the Duchess, she observed, had once been very rudely treated by a purser on an Atlantic liner, which she apparently regarded as a sufficient reason for distrusting pursers as a class, and disregarding their advice.

"I do think you're so wise, Lady Mary," said Mrs. Burslem, "and of course the Duchess would be likely to know best in such matters! I must say I don't much like the look of the purser myself; he made a great fuss about changing £100 for me the other day into Greek coinage: one does like to have a little money with one—it's so very inconvenient not being able to buy any little thing one sees. I should like to show you some draperies I bought at Taormina—such a bargain, too, you'd hardly believe it, but I only gave £60 for them!"

Lady Mary, an impecunious aristocrat, who privately disliked both Mrs. Burslem and the whole class to which she so obviously belonged, closed her eyes in a manner which might no doubt have been taken for approval of her neighbour's acumen, but really

The Second Shock

represented horror at her extravagance, and a sense of the indecency of discussing prices in public.

The archdeacons were not slow to see a connection between the purser's notice and their own private adventure.

"That seems to clear things up a bit," said the Archdeacon of Thorp. "This woman, whoever she is, who thinks she knows me (if that *is* what she thinks) must evidently have got wind of some rogue on board, and went to the purser or the captain, which she'd have done at first if she'd had any sense. Now she'll be happy, and we can rest in peace."

"I do hope you are right," said Archdeacon Castleton. "What a pity it is that young women are so impulsive!"

"Oh, she was young, was she?" asked Craggs. "I thought you said you hardly saw her."

"I did not," replied Castleton, hastily and with emphasis. "I was only thinking that it sounded rather a youthful performance."

"Well, anyhow, it's a relief to know it wasn't a female admirer either of yours or mine! Really, there ought to be special measures taken to protect the clergy from the female sex: when I was a curate, I was pestered with slippers, and nowadays I'm always having to try and keep my young clergy from getting entangled—not with much success, I'm afraid."

"It is not only curates," said Castleton, with a heartfelt sigh. "There was a lady not long ago who wrote to one of the archbishops, addressing him as 'His Disgrace the Arch-Fiend', pretending that he had trifled with her affections."

"Then there was that other lady who threw a prayer-book at the canon in St. Paul's," chimed in Craggs.

"Even gaiters are not an adequate protection nowadays," said Castleton, emphatically.

"Oh, you've had it too, have you?" said the Archdeacon of Thorp: "anyhow, it's a comfort to know we're pretty safe from it here."

The Second Shock

They joined in mutual congratulations; but their content was destined to be of short duration. That very night, when they retired to rest, well pleased with a triumph which they had achieved together at the bridge table, they found a note lying on the floor of their cabin: it bore the simple address, J.C.

"Here's a letter for you, Castleton," said Craggs, who was the first to see it.

The Archdeacon of Garminster picked it up.

"It may just as well be for you," he remarked: "our initials are the same."

"Quite true," said his friend, "it looks as if we should have to toss again: you shall do the tossing this time: fair play's a jewel!"

Castleton tossed accordingly. This time the luck was with him: and Craggs took the note.

"Very well," he said, "I'll open it, but without prejudice, mind! The mere opening proves nothing."

He read the note and handed it to his brother archdeacon.

"It seems to be for you after all," he said.

The Ven. James Castleton took the note and read it in his turn. It ran:

"I want you to know that your secret is safe with me. You can be sure that I will not betray you. How I love to think that we have this little secret—just between our two selves!"

It was written in an unmistakably feminine hand: there was no signature.

CHAPTER IV

The Third Shock

"Thou art turned the greatest liar."
—SHAKESPEARE

The two friends gazed blankly at one another. An observer might have noticed that, while the faces of both were flushed, in the one case it was by the blush of outraged modesty, in the other is was the unmistakable glow of anger. Their first remarks would have confirmed this diagnosis.

"How extremely tiresome!" said the Archdeacon of Garminster, "but I do not see why you were so sure that it was meant for me."

"Confound the woman!" said the Archdeacon of Thorp, who was privately by no means so certain. "I should like to wring her neck!"

"I suppose you do not think," began Castleton, tentatively, "I suppose you do not think it would be a good plan to give up all attempt at disguise? After all, it is not very important, is it? Would there be any harm in letting the facts be known?"

"Of course you can do just as you like," returned Craggs, who, as we have already suggested, was made of sterner stuff. "I'm certainly not going to alter my arrangements just because of a silly letter like this. As you say, it isn't really very important, and it would be fairly simple for you, but I've been going about as if I were a layman, and I should look uncommonly silly if I suddenly said I was an archdeacon after all: I don't think people would like it—you know how stuffy they are—and anyhow, I'm not going to be made to look a fool just because some hysterical idiot chooses to write an anonymous letter."

"I wonder if it is still the same lady?" said Castleton.

"I don't see any reason why it should be," returned Craggs. "There's no necessary connection between writing anonymous letters and making assignations by night—but on the other hand it does suggest much the same sort of mentality. I can't help thinking that most likely it's that original acquaintance of yours, the woman who you thought seemed to know you, I mean. If so, that's all the more reason why I shouldn't let it affect me."

"We couldn't find her out by the handwriting, I suppose?" suggested the Archdeacon of Garminster.

"Not a chance of it; we couldn't very well go round asking all the female passengers for their autographs; besides, she writes just that silly characterless hand which so many girls pick up in schools. We can keep our eyes open and that's about all we can do."

Archdeacon Castleton gave vent to a heavy sigh. He could not deny the force of his companion's arguments, but the idea of "keeping his eyes open", on the off-chance that he might some day encounter an answering glance of intelligence from a feminine eye, was one which made singularly little appeal to a person of his modest disposition.

"There's only one good thing about the business," said Craggs, "which is that no one else can know anything about the letter; so, if we do nothing, we may reasonably hope that we shall hear no more about it."

But even this modest satisfaction was only to be briefly theirs. When they came down to breakfast next morning, they found the Wilsons already consuming their grape-fruit.

"Good morning," said Wilson. "Looks like being another good day, doesn't it? By the way, I hope you got your letter all right, last night?"

The Third Shock

The archdeacons cast a mute glance of dismay at one another, but, not noticing it, Wilson went on: "I went into your cabin last night to see if I could borrow that guide book you were talking about, and I couldn't help seeing a note lying on the floor; it seemed rather an untidy place for it, and I nearly picked it up, but I thought I'd better not be too officious, so I just left it there."

Archdeacon Castleton was incapable of speech, being fully occupied with that hardest of all tasks, that of trying to suppress an insistent blush, but his colleague was equal to the occasion.

"Oh yes, thank you, I found it all right; it wasn't at all important—only a note from a friend on board."

"Oh, have you got a friend on board?" said Mrs. Wilson, brightly. "I thought you said you didn't know anyone and didn't much want to. I remember I thought it was horrid of you to be so unsociable!"

"He only came on at Toulon," said Craggs, with a rapid glance at Castleton: "he's been lying low for reasons of his own."

"A mysterious stranger," cried Mrs. Wilson, girlishly, "how exciting! Then I'm afraid we shan't see him going about with you."

"No, I'm afraid not," said the archdeacon. "He wants to keep to himself. I'm afraid I can't tell you his reasons, for he wants them kept private."

"Don't be so inquisitive, Mary," said her husband. "You ought to know that everyone isn't as gregarious as you are! Which reminds me, who's that Continental-looking chap you were going about with yesterday?"

"Oh, Mr. Michalis, do you mean? He's so nice, he was so polite to poor old Lady Mary the other day when she couldn't manage the little jump from the boat on to the gangway."

"Don't like Dagoes myself," said Mr. Wilson. "Funny word—dago. By the way, anyone know where it comes from?"

The Third Shock

Mr. Birtley, who had just made his appearance, was ready with an answer.

"The term is only properly applied to Spaniards," he said, "and is, I understand, a corruption of the word Diego, which is itself derived from Sant Iago, the patron saint of Spain."

"What a thing it is to be well informed," said Wilson, admiringly: "and what about Wops? Can you throw any light on them?"

"The term Wop is, I fear, beyond my powers of elucidation," replied Mr. Birtley: "but I fancy that your friend, Mr. Michalis, if (as I am credibly informed) he *is* a Greek, might not improperly, though impolitely, be so described."

"I don't think I'll try it on him," said Wilson. "I've an idea he might not altogether like it."

"I regard 'Limey' as a very objectionable word," put in Mr. Pycroft, who was the last to arrive.

"Oh, who are 'Limeys'?" asked Mrs. Wilson. "They don't sound at all nice."

"You're one yourself, my dear, and so am I," said her husband. "That's what the Americans call all the English, but heaven only knows why!"

"Far be it from me to claim an equality with the celestial powers," said Mr. Birtley, "but I can in this case supply an answer to the question. The British sailor used to be provided with lime juice to minimise the ravages of scurvy, and the name was given them, whether in envy or in contempt I am not sure, by their American rivals."

"What a horrid drink to be called after!" said Mrs. Wilson. "They might at least have called us after beer or cider, or something respectable like that! I do think we're much nicer in the names we give to other people."

"Well, I can't say I think either Wop or Dago is particularly attractive as a name," said her husband, "but at any rate we don't call the Americans anything worse than Yanks."

"I was in America during Prohibition," said Mr. Pycroft, who was always showing a surprising range of experience, "and I drank so much tomato juice by way of cocktails that I never wish to taste it again."

"It doesn't strike one as very exhilarating," said Wilson.

"It depressed me, all right," said Mr. Pycroft.

"With admirable moderation", remarked Mr. Birtley, "we refrained in those days from calling them 'Tomatys' which would have been a reasonable retaliation for 'Limeys'. I confess that I dislike the thought that, if I were to visit the United States, I should infallibly be described in their papers as a 'Limey Prof.'"

"Well, Michalis may be all right, whether he's a Wop or not," said Wilson, returning to the original point, "but I must say I've no use at all for his pal Blades."

"Shocking bounder," grunted Mr. Pycroft.

"Oh but, Jack, they aren't friends at all!" protested Mrs. Wilson. "It's only that they have to share a cabin, and poor Mr. Michalis can't very well shake him off. He's so kind-hearted—that's what I really like him for—he doesn't want to hurt Mr. Blades's feelings."

"I don't believe he's got any feelings," said her husband, "at any rate I'm sure he's got none I should at all mind hurting myself."

Neither archdeacons had taken any part in this discussion: their thoughts, it may be surmised, were far away, with the nameless *inamorata* whose missive had troubled their repose. The Archdeacon of Garminster felt some slight qualms at his friend's lapse from veracity, though he was unable to deny that his fertility of invention had rescued them both from a somewhat awkward situation.

"You acted on the principle *Pecca fortiter*," he observed, when they were alone, "and I confess that I realized to the full the wisdom of your action. I shudder to think what would have happened if Mrs. Wilson had learnt what the letter contained! It would have been all over the boat in less than no time."

"She's a very determined talker," agreed his colleague. "It's a comfort to think we've staved off her curiosity for a bit; that's why I said what I did about 'private reasons', though I should have been hard put to it to explain exactly what they were, if she'd pressed the point; but luckily she's got some sense of decency. It's just as well we're to have a day ashore. I'm really looking forward to seeing Crete."

"In the peculiar circumstances of the moment, there could be no more appropriate place for a call," said the Archdeacon of Garminster, demurely.

"What on earth do you mean? Why is Crete so appropriate?"

"I hardly like to suggest it," proceeded Castleton, more slily still, "but it occurred to me to wonder whether it was possible that you may find in Crete your spiritual home."

"I haven't the least idea what you're driving at," said Craggs.

"We have sound apostolic evidence for the belief that the Cretans were always liars!" said the Archdeacon of Garminster.

CHAPTER V

A Day in Crete

"There was a sound of revelry."
—BYRON

Meanwhile the general life of the boat had continued on lines which will be familiar to all who have taken part in such cruises. The ship's bores, all unconscious of their reputation, had selected their prey: their victims, all too conscious of their own weakness, had resigned themselves to their fate, and, half fascinated and half resentful, listened to interminable discourses

A Day in Crete

on topics of the mildest interest. The lusty games players had established a prescriptive right to play deck-tennis or shuffleboard at all the most suitable places and at all the most convenient times, so that timid novices hastened apologetically to conclude their amateurish efforts. The ladies who did embroidery had entered into a defensive alliance against those who could only knit, while those who prided themselves on their powers of composition had established a lien on the only tables at which there was a supply of ink.

The passengers were beginning to know one another: the sight of a particular book on a chair was sufficient proof of its absent occupier: no one but Mr. Michalis was likely to be reading Balzac, and *Mycenean Man* revealed the proximity of Miss Bustard. It became safe to assume that Mr. Wilbraham, whose flamboyant dressing-gown had caused some scandal, would, if the weather permitted, be teaching Miss Carruthers to sunbathe on the boat-deck, and that, whatever the weather conditions might be, Professor Tomkins would be preparing a lecture and Lady Mary Culham would be asleep. The cruise, in other words, was proving a success.

Our particular friends presented few problems to their fellow passengers: the Wilsons were easy to place, and were equally at home in the smoking room or in the more decorous atmosphere of the drawing room: it was easy to see in Mr. Castleton one of those scholarly country clergy who have been, since Chaucer's day, the pride of their country. Mr. Birtley, the obvious schoolmaster abroad, was regarded with that tolerant distaste which the English show for the inevitable: Mr. Pycroft and Mr. Craggs were the only two who offered any field for speculation. The former was at first believed to be a don, on the strength of a correction he had made of one of the Professor's wilder utterances, but when a conversation in the smoking room revealed him as knowing all the Derby winners of the last half century they (like the inhabitants of Malta when they first saw St. Paul) changed their minds and regarded him not exactly "as a god", but as the *Lucretia*'s walking encyclopædia. Craggs had been diagnosed at first as a man from Scotland Yard on a holiday, but when it was realized that he was reading detective stories without visible disapproval, this conjecture was rejected as untenable; a certain incisiveness of utterance favoured the assumption that he was a barrister in large practice, and there were those who claimed to have often seen his name in the Law Reports.

The judicious, or at any rate the charitable, reader will be slow to complain that no "events" disturbed the passage of the *Lucretia* through Mediterranean waters. Enveloped in that soothing atmosphere of her own which we have endeavoured to describe, secure from contact with the outside world, the good ship sped on her way, little dreaming of the perils which the mainland held, nor fearing that the islands held at least a presage of disaster.

In the absence of events, all we can do is to record some fragments of a conversation which may prove to have been not without a bearing on what was soon to befall her.

The Wilsons, Miss Bustard and Mr. Michalis had drifted together in a corner of the smoking room, and after a little the conversation turned, not unnaturally, to the purser's warning notice.

"Nasty to think we've got a criminal on board," observed Mr. Wilson.

"I cannot say that I am altogether surprised," said Miss Bustard, in acid tones.

"Oh, Miss Bustard," cried Mrs. Wilson, excitedly, "you don't mean to say..."

"I do not mean to say anything," replied Miss Bustard, "except that if one keeps one's eyes and one's ears open, it is clear that everyone on this boat is not what he appears to be."

Mrs. Wilson cast a glance at her husband.

"Jack and I thought that too, didn't we?"

"Oh, nonsense, Mary! I can't have you talking scandal."

"I have no sort of desire to talk scandal, or to listen to it," said Miss Bustard, severely, "but when one sees Mr. Wilbraham in a passage where he could have no business..."

Mrs. Wilson gave a little yelp of excitement. "Oh, how thrilling! What passage was it, Miss Bustard?"

"It was the passage to the cabins of Lady Mary Culham and Mrs. Burslem."

"You spotted him all right?" asked Jack Wilson.

Miss Bustard obviously disliked the word.

"I know Mr. Wilbraham's dressing-gown only too well," she replied.

"But you wouldn't suspect him of being a thief, would you?"

"No one is beyond suspicion," said Miss Bustard, severely.

"Not even the Professor?" put in Wilson, with a laugh.

"A man who deliberately falsifies facts", said Miss Bustard, "would, in my opinion, be capable of any iniquity."

Mr. Wilson was far from anxious to be led into a discussion of the Professor's blunders: he turned to Michalis. "Your stable companion—what's his name? Blades, isn't it?—has a poorish press, I gather."

"Ah, my faith," said Michalis with a sigh. "He is in truth capable of everything, that one! I ask myself often what he does in this galley. He has no friends, that understands itself, and for the antiquities, he regards them not at all. For me, I speak with him as little as may be. But for the crime, the ability lacks: he is of a stupidity immense, unbelievable!"

"Well, that's a comfort anyway," said Wilson. "Still, I'm glad to think you'll have your eye on him: he'll be sure to give himself away."

And, indeed, the landing on Crete was to reveal Mr. Blades in a singularly unprepossessing light.

A Day in Crete

On the island of Crete, or rather in its vicinity, Professor Tomkins was in his element. The Lion of Venice on the harbour mouth gave him the opportunity of explaining how widely the Venetian dominions had once extended, and of making a learned digression on Ragusa, the only port on the east of the Adriatic which had never owned her sway. This in turn led to an excursus on the derivation of the word "argosy" from the city's name, and there were moments when it seemed reasonable to fear that he would deal exhaustively with the history of Mediterranean trade through the centuries.

It may have been the disapproving eye of Miss Bustard which warned him off from such a project, but even that piercing organ had no power to lure him back from the Adriatic to Crete, the professed subject of his lecture. A reasoned lament on the cruel fate which now called Ragusa "Dubrovnik" led naturally to a protest against Spalato being called Split, and, having by this device led his hearers to Spalato (whither it is to be feared he had always meant to take them), he treated them to a disquisition on the first appearance in architecture of an arch mounted on a column in the colonnade outside Diocletian's palace, and a description (illustrated by photographs) of Mestrovic's colossal statue of Gregory of Nin, which completely dwarfed the cathedral.

Some slight signs of restiveness in his audience, which felt it had been gathered together on somewhat false pretences, was momentarily appeased by an anecdote about two magnificent Dalmatian dogs, which proved to have been bred in Birmingham and not in the country from which they took their name, but time was drawing short, and the Professor driven in the end to explain that this was only a preliminary discourse, to be followed by another on the next night. His audience dispersed, having learnt little definite about Crete, except that there was, as he had told them in his opening sentence, a Venetian Lion on the wall at the harbour's mouth.

"He reminds me forcibly", said Craggs who, contrary to his usual custom, had been among the audience, "of the man who introduced a speaker at such enormous length that he found when he had finished his remarks that the lecturer had had to leave to catch the last train home."

"Lady Mary got a good sleep anyhow," said Wilson; "it's a pity she's got such a shrill snore."

"I remember once being asked to preach before the University of Cambridge," said Archdeacon Castleton, "and one of the Heads of Colleges was snoring loudly before I had finished giving out my text."

"Showed there wasn't anything personal about it, anyhow!" said Wilson.

"No, that was certainly a comfort. The Cambridge pulpit, as it happens, is on rails, and it occurred to me that it might be a useful device to have the pulpit and the preacher automatically withdrawn after a reasonable interval: possibly the same plan might with advantage be adopted with lecturers who exceeded their time limit."

"Good idea!" said Wilson. "When I was at school there was a sort of sounding-board thing over the pulpit, and I used often to think what fun it would be if it was gradually lowered, so that a chap who went on too long would have to squeak out his last sentences through the little crack that was left."

"I fancy it would take more than a little thing like that to discourage Professor Tomkins," said the Archdeacon of Thorp. "I observe there's to be another lecture on Crete to-morrow."

"Not to me, anyhow," said Wilson.

"Your attitude", said Mr. Birtley, who had joined them in the smoking room, "reminds me of the American story of the long-winded preacher who (after dealing exhaustively with most of the Minor Prophets) exclaimed, 'Where, my friends, where shall we place Hosea?' and was somewhat disconcerted to hear a

A Day in Crete

member of the congregation exclaim, 'You can place Hosea right here, sir—I'm off!' "

The second lecture on Crete was duly delivered, though, for reasons which will perhaps have become obvious, the audience was somewhat smaller. In it, the Professor did full justice to the prehistoric situation and to the amazing discoveries of Sir Arthur Evans; gave a sketch of the native religions, skated delicately over the question how the Cretan harbour, at which St. Paul hoped to stay, managed to lie "towards the S.W. and the N.W."; and concluded with a review of Cretan history from the earliest times to the present day.

"My, but he covers the ground!" quoted a student of Kipling, when some of the audience were later gathered in the smoking room. "I will say this for old Tomkins, he doesn't spare himself—or us!"

"I wish he'd said a bit more about Venizelos," said an ex-M.P. called Ryland. "He did just say he came from Crete, but he might have given us a bit more about him. I remember there used to be some goodish yarns about him and his opponents. One was that his political enemies plotted to have him assassinated when he was Prime Minister, but couldn't agree how much they ought to pay the assassin when he only winged him; and then, when he was out of office, there was another yarn how they arrested his godson (I think it was) and sentenced him to death, but the Cretans sent a message to say that, if he was killed, they'd decided to assassinate the Governor of Crete. As you know, the Cretans haven't any too good a reputation for truthfulness, but the Government thought this was a promise they would most certainly keep, so they had to let the chap go!"

"He might have said a bit more about the roads we built when we were in the island," put in an R.E. major. "Crete and Corfu used to be the only places in Greece where there were roads

A Day in Crete

one could drive on—of course they've built some since, but I'm talking of twenty years ago."

"Yes, I remember when it was a pretty serious job driving from the Piraeus to Athens," said Ryland.

"There's another thing about Corfu," put in Craggs. "I've seen the children there playing cricket in the streets—that's something you'd hardly find anywhere else in Europe outside the British Isles."

"Ah, that dates back to old Sir Thomas Maitland—King Tom, as they used to call him," said the Major. "It's a fine island, Corfu: it's a great pity old Gladstone induced us to give it back to the Greeks."

But here the conversation drifted into politics, and lost its local interest.

The day for Crete at last arrived, and there was a smooth sea for their passage to the island, though there were sinister tales of tourists who had been caught by a gale while on shore, and had had to spend a very uncomfortable night in very uncongenial quarters.

"Nice-looking young chap, that Second Officer," said Craggs to Pycroft, as they sat together in the bows.

"So the young ladies seem to think," was the cynical answer.

"I remember an awkward episode", went on Pycroft, "when I was on a Yugoslav boat years ago. All the Yugoslav officers were as handsome as the devil: they sat there like graven images, and the young ladies got it into their heads that they knew no English. So they jabbered away, saying how beautiful the chap in the stern was, and chaffing one another about him. You should have seen their faces when they heard him giving instructions when they landed, all in perfect English."

The travellers, as we know, had been intellectually well prepared for their trip, and they spent a pleasant and profitable day on the island, inspecting the excavations at Knossos and the reconstructions in the museum, getting glimpses of golden orioles in the trees, and sampling Malmsey wine, not from the wood but from the bottle.

This last amusement had a distressing sequel, for Mr. Blades, no doubt through inattention to the Professor's lecture (if indeed he attended it, which is more than doubtful) failed to realize the strength of the local beverage, and passed with surprising celerity through the belligerent, the amatory and the lachrymose stages of intoxication. In the first, he was with difficulty restrained from offering physical violence to Professor Tomkins, whose nose he repeatedly expressed the desire to punch; in the second, he made most unwelcome advances to Miss Bustard who, though not herself (as we know) a devotee of the Professor, had come most gallantly to his assistance, when she saw the cause of Learning attacked in his person; and in the third, he lowered the spirits of the party by a loud and lamentable rendering of "Just a Song at Twilight" when they had begun to head for home.

To spare the feelings of Lady Mary who, deaf as she was, could not fail to perceive that some funereal dirge was being rendered, it was thought wise to tell her that poor Mr. Blades had just received some very bad news from home; but the well-meant precaution failed in its purpose. Unexpectedly and unfortunately, the news effected a permanent lodgment in her mind, and next day, with a graciousness quite unusual with her, she was moved to offer her sympathy, saying that she was sure that sightseeing went ill with an aching heart.

"It ain't so much the 'eart, your ladyship, as the blinkin' 'ead!" was Mr. Blades's unexpected reply. Fortunately Miss Hillcroft was at hand to deal with the situation, and to receive bitter and quite unmerited reproaches, on having led her employer into so unfortunate a conversation.

A Day in Crete

General sympathy was felt and expressed with Mr. Michalis for the close association with the delinquent into which circumstances had forced him, and even the charity of the Archdeacon of Garminster could not deny that Mr. Blades was far from showing that single-minded interest in Greek antiquities which might be reasonably expected from a member of the Hellenic Travellers' Club.

Mrs. Wilson, as might have been expected, was loud in her sympathy for Mr. Michalis.

"I do like him so much," she said, "and I love that funny way he talks English—half of it really French, you know! When I talk French in that same sort of way, no French people ever seem to like it a bit, but I think it's very attractive in him—it's such fun listening to see what French idiom he'll use next. He's told me a lot about that horrid Blades: he really hates him like poison, though he's too kind-hearted to say so. But don't let's talk about him any more! I want to get on with my cross-word: Jack is so helpless—he's really no use at all!"

"Oh, come, Mary!" said her husband, "I did something for you only yesterday!"

"Oh, yes! a horrid cricketing thing—'Disgruntled bowler's place in the field': how *could* I know that was 'Long off'?"

"She doesn't know the first thing about cricket: would you believe it, I had to tell her that Trumper was 'A card-playing batsman'? I can't think what they teach young women nowadays."

"Anyhow, this isn't anything about cricket: 'Bird suggesting High Church doctrine in Herefordshire'—nine letters: you ought to know that, Mr. Castleton!"

"I thought that was your part of the world, Mrs. Wilson," said Castleton, smiling: "I am afraid it is quite beyond me!"

"Have you got any letters?" asked Craggs.

"Yes, there's a T in the middle and it ends with an S."

"Oh, 'Albatross', surely," said Craggs.

"Oh, how clever of you, Mr. Craggs! Now I shall know where to come when I'm in trouble; but don't you think Mr. Castleton ought to have guessed it?"

"Albs are uncommon in my part of the world," said the archdeacon, a little severely, "and I fear that I am even more incompetent than your husband: I sometimes glance at the children's cross-word in the *Daily Mail*, but even that is beyond my capacity."

When he and Craggs were alone, he expressed himself with some acerbity.

"I did not at all like the look she gave me," he said. "I suppose there is no possibility that she knows who I am?"

"Oh, I don't think so: she knows you are a parson, of course, and that's enough for her. I shouldn't worry about it, if I were you."

"I only trust that you are right," said the Archdeacon of Garminster with a sigh. "But I certainly did *not* like the way she looked at me."

CHAPTER VI

Sidelights on Politics

"Stop, let me have the truth of that!"
—BROWNING

But it was no doubt the obvious benevolence of Archdeacon Castleton which caused Mr. Michalis to select him as his chief *confidant* and to pour his troubles into his sympathetic ear. He did so with a wealth of gesture and a profusion of Gallic idioms which made it clear that he had learnt his English on a foreign soil. In the course of their long conversation it became plain that Mrs. Wilson had by no means exaggerated in saying that Blades was very far from being his soul-mate: it seemed indeed, as the archdeacon said afterwards, that it was rather one of those cases to which St. Paul referred when he spoke of a man "unequally yoked with an unbeliever".

It appeared that, so far from being responsible for Blades, he had never seen or heard of him till he found him ensconced in the cabin which they shared, where he had characteristically appropriated the more commodious bunk.

"That is his way of acting, Monsieur Castleton! It is without doubt a small thing, but he lacks entirely—oh, but entirely—the consideration! He lacks—it pains me to say it—but he lacks completely the sentiments of a gentleman, and his manners! They are of a grossness inconceivable! In the cabin he leaves everything above-below, what you call higgle-piggledy, and at the table he behaves himself to make cry out! And his language—it is all that there is of least decent! You have heard, is it not? of what he has said to the poor Lady Mary, a lady most respectable and of a kindness of heart!—and for the *tohu-bohu* on the island, it is enough to make blush even to think of it!"

Castleton's sympathetic murmurs encouraged him to continue.

"To live with such a man day by day, it is a trial of the most extreme: for me, I do my possible, but it demands a patience,—a fortitude—that sees itself. And for me too, there is another difficulty of the most grave: me, I am a patriot Greek: I love my poor country, and would wish to help her, but he, it is not only that he regards her not at all, but that, as I fear, he allies himself, in what way I know not, with all that is least wise in the life political. Me, for certain, I know nothing, but he has associations of the least desirable, and I fear that when we come to Athens, he will seek to renew them. What then is my duty? You see in what trouble I find myself, and that is why I seek the counsel of such a man as yourself, Monsieur."

The archdeacon was beginning to protest his own incapacity to give any valuable opinion on Greek politics, but Michalis silenced him with a gesture, and went on volubly:

"And even that, Monsieur, that is not all! I fear greatly that he is not himself an honest man! I say it with much reserve, for I am not one who likes to speak evil—not at all—and you would not wish it, you who are a man of religion. But to have spoken to such a man, it will be for me a lightening of the conscience: I make, one may say it, the confession!"

Castleton, who was not himself in the habit of hearing confessions, gave an inward shiver: he tried feebly to suggest that someone like Craggs might be a more useful recipient of Michalis' confidence, but the suggestion was brushed aside.

"Ah, Monsieur Craggs! I have for him a great respect: he is an honourable man, that sees itself—but of a severity, of a hardness! It is to you, Monsieur, a priest, that I address myself. For this Blades, I fear much that he is little better than a thief! I have seen him regard the jewels of Mrs. Burslem—she is a type, that one, is it not so?—but regard her jewels with an eye of longing, and he has let fall now and then a little word which makes to wonder if he has not designs—of what sort, I know not, I—but it gives furiously to think. What then to do? To go to the Captain? But I have nothing sure to tell, and he will mock himself of me: to approach myself to this Madame Burslem? But she will laugh me to the nose and will not trouble herself of my suspicions. And so I speak to you, Monsieur Castleton, a man of whom the visage is full both of piety and of wisdom. I speak to you, and of you I demand what counsel you have to give, in an affair so anxious and of an ambiguity so extreme!"

The Archdeacon of Garminster, like most Englishmen, had a very hazy idea of the laws concerning libel and slander, except for an uneasy conviction that the truer a charge might be, the more dangerous it was to make it in public. Accordingly, he hummed and hawed about the suggestion of Blades's criminal intentions, saying that he would have to think the matter over very carefully, and would take an early opportunity of seeing Michalis again. By way of making up for his temporary failure, as a counsellor, he encouraged him to go on talking about Greek politics, which seemed a comparatively safe subject, and Blades's possible connection with them. Michalis was only too ready to discourse on this theme, and in the course of half an hour, the archdeacon had accumulated a great deal of intimate (and very possibly inaccurate) information concerning the current affairs of the Kingdom of the Hellenes.

According to Michalis, as he afterwards told Archdeacon Craggs, the King had made up his mind, when he returned to Greece from England, that he must have a really honest election: this was rather a difficult matter to arrange, for nothing of the kind had ever been heard of in Greece, and the suggestion, when first made, was exceedingly unpopular. However, the King got his way and the election was duly held, in reasonable accordance with the best British traditions. Then his bad luck began.

"There were two parties, it seems," said Castleton, "the one Royalist and the other Republican, and most unfortunately both of them secured exactly the same number of seats—I forget how many they were, but that makes no difference. The point is that, as they were exactly equal, the casting vote lay with a little party of about half a dozen Communists who came from Kavalla, the place where most of the Greek tobacco is grown. I have no idea why growing tobacco should turn a man into a Communist, and Michalis did not try to explain it to me, but there seems to be no doubt that it does have that effect in Greece."

Mr. Birtley had been listening to Castleton's exposition.

"To see the result of one's labours literally go up in smoke", he said, "could hardly fail to have a demoralizing effect upon the character, and might well encourage an extravagant demand for a New Order!"

"Well, that was how things stood when a queer thing happened. According to Michalis (who is inclined, I gather, to be a Royalist himself—but I think his account is quite impartial), according to him, all the Royalists were only Royalists because they expected the King to make it worth their while, and give them the official pickings, as one may say, so, as soon as they found that he meant to do nothing of the kind, they all with one consent became Republicans. On the other hand, the Republicans were so pleased with him for taking that attitude that they all became Royalists—so there they were, with the situation as difficult as before and party government still impossible. As there was no point in Parliament's meeting, the King put in a prime minister who was just a good business man, and all went well until he died, which was a second bit of bad luck for the King. So then he called in Metaxas."

"Bit of a dark horse, Metaxas," put in Pycroft. "They call him the silkworm—I don't know why!"

"Nor do I," said Castleton. "I do not think Michalis did either, at any rate he did not tell me, if he did—but he said that if you were on his side you showed it by wearing silk socks or a silk shirt or a silk tie, and if you left any of them off it was a sign that you had gone over to the Opposition. I do hope", he added, "that all this is not boring you dreadfully. I confess that I found it extremely interesting, as he told it to me, but naturally I have no means of judging how much of it is accurate!"

"It's not a bit boring," said Craggs. "Do carry on! Did he leave you under the impression that Metaxas' government was efficient?"

"Oh, yes, perhaps even a little too efficient, if anything: the opposition seems to have been driven underground, or, perhaps it would be truer to say, up into the mountains, where there are a good lot of brigands who call themselves Liberals. Michalis clearly has no sympathy with them, and thinks they are really much more interested in plunder than in politics. Anyhow those are the people he thinks Blades may be connected with, but he admits that his ideas are very vague, and he was anxious to make it clear that he could not prove anything of the kind against him. I formed quite a good opinion of Michalis himself: he was very anxious that I should not assume that his suspicions were certainly justified, and also to be fair to Blades, although one could see that he had little doubt himself. It was a very interesting but a somewhat exhausting afternoon," concluded the archdeacon, mopping his brow, for it was a hot day, "and I am glad to think that all this political business is no affair of mine."

"But what about the thieving side of it?" asked Craggs. "He seems to have made you his father-confessor about that."

"Might drop the purser a hint," said Pycroft, "couldn't do any harm—name no names of course, just tell him we think his notice went round just in time."

"Yes, that might encourage him to go on keeping his eyes open," said Craggs. "I don't see we can do any more, and I don't think we ought to do less."

It was agreed that Pycroft should take an early opportunity of seeing the purser.

"You *will* be very careful not to bring Michalis into it, won't you?" pleaded Archdeacon Castleton, who was somewhat daunted by the recollection of an action for slander from which he had had hard work to save a too-outspoken vicar. "I promised him faithfully that I would not give him away, and I should not at all like him to think that I had betrayed his confidence."

"That'll be all right," said Pycroft.

"Thank you very much, and now I think I really must go and have a rest: his English is so queer that it really was something of a strain to follow what he was saying."

And the archdeacon departed to seek peace and repose.

"Though, as Castleton was saying, it's really no business of ours," said Archdeacon Craggs, "I think it might be interesting to follow up the line of Blades's political activities, if we get the chance. If there's anything in what Michalis says, he'll be likely to try to get in touch with his disreputable friends when we get to Athens."

"I should like, parenthetically", said Mr. Birtley, "to thank you for avoiding the use of that deplorable word 'contact', which is so often and so distressingly employed as a verb nowadays."

"I'm much obliged," said Craggs. "One of my clergy said he hoped to 'contact me' the other day, and I felt bound to tell him I hoped he'd do nothing of the sort. But, as I say, I think we might do worse than keep an eye on his proceedings in Athens, just in case."

"Might be worth doing," agreed Pycroft.

"Speaking for myself," said Mr. Birtley, "I cannot say that I feel myself to be possessed of any of the essential attributes of the successful sleuth."

"Might quite well be amusing," said Pycroft. "I'm quite ready to play, if you like."

"I don't see", said Craggs, "how Blades could have any suspicions of you or me as being on his trail; it isn't as if it were Castleton: he's sure to have noticed Michalis having that long talk with him: and, as far as he's concerned, he may have got the wind up, for he must know Michalis' opinion of him—but we're safe enough."

"Right," said Pycroft, "then we'll have a shot: it's no good making plans till we see how things arrange themselves in Athens. It may be rather tricky, if there are a lot of separate expeditions: easy for him to slip off by himself: but we'll hope for the best."

And on this understanding the friends separated.

CHAPTER VII

Sleuths in Athens

> "Trace this alley up and down."
> —Shakespeare

On the arrival of the *Lucretia* in Athens, it was found that fortune favoured the amateur sleuths. Owing to some difficulty about the supply of taxis, it was decided to postpone any of the longer expeditions till the second day, and the Hellenic Travellers were supplied with railway tickets for the short journey from the Piraeus, where the ship lay, into Athens itself. It was easy for Craggs and Pycroft to secure a seat in the same carriage as Mr. Blades, and to follow his movements without any risk of arousing his suspicions.

While most of the party directed their course either to the Acropolis, or the Museum, according to their desire to hear, or to avoid hearing, the discourses which Professor Tomkins proposed to deliver in the morning and afternoon at these places respectively, Blades apparently had other views. After travelling as far as the train would take him, he got out and bent his steps up a small street close by.

"Shoe Lane," said Pycroft, who had once, it now appeared spent a fortnight at the British School at Athens, though it was characteristic of him that he had not previously referred to it.

"Good place for old shops," he observed, as they prepared to follow in Blades's steps"—about the best in Athens—mostly junk, of course, but you may pick up something worth having, if you have luck. Means a rare lot of bargaining, though. As no one has the least idea what the drachma's really worth from day to day, it's a bit tricky for both sides."

They followed Blades up the street, resisting the temptation to investigate the icons and pieces of embroidery which many of the shops displayed. Half-way up the Lane he met an unattractive-looking little Greek whom he appeared to know. It seemed that he was asking his way, for the Greek waved his arms and pointed up the street. After a few minutes' talk they separated and Blades pursued his way.

Towards the top of the street he turned into a shop, which, like many of the rest, displayed the large and varied assortment of footwear from which the Lane took its name.

"No more we can do now," said Pycroft. "Can't very well go in and buy boots; not quite your style, perhaps!"

"No, I think not," said Craggs decidedly, "but I suppose it would be worth while to find out whose shop it is."

"Yes, I'll see to that, I know the chap next door; used to get things from him sometimes when I was here: a fearful old rascal, but rather a friend of mine: he'll give me the name, then I'll go along and look up a man at the British School, and see if anything's known about him: my chap's by way of being an expert on Greek politics—been here digging about ten years. You'd better go off and see the sights."

Craggs, who had only paid one short visit to Athens several years before, was glad to be released from his detective duties and made his way to the Acropolis, where he found, somewhat to his relief, that the lecture was over and the party abandoned to its own devices. He was able to rescue the Archdeacon of Garminster from the clutches of Mrs. Burslem, into which his kindness of heart had allowed him to fall, and to save him from hearing the conclusion of a discourse in which the Parthenon was compared, considerably to its disadvantage, with the Manchester Town Hall.

"It's not what I would call a homely place, Mr. Castleton," she was saying, "and, by all that I can see, the draughts must have been something terrible, and no one can deny it is in a shocking state of repair. But there, what can you expect of a country where no one seems to know what their own coins are worth? I know what I should say if someone told me they didn't know if a florin was worth £2 or 2d.—but this drachma, or whatever they call it, seems to go jumping about till no one knows what it was worth yesterday or what it'll be worth to-morrow. Most unbusinesslike, I call it."

Earnest young ladies were tripping about, *Bædeker* in hand, verifying the points to which the Professor had directed their attention: the more youthful, active and irresponsible members of the party were investigating the possibility of scaling the rock from various angles. Cameras were being busily used, and here and there an artist was hurriedly committing to paper some of the more famous of the buildings, or trying to do justice to the glorious view through the Propylaea.

"I believe moonlight's really the best time to see it," said Craggs, "just as Walter Scott so wisely remarked about Melrose. I've never managed it myself, but I hope we may be able to pull it off this time—but I don't know if the moon's in a good temper at the moment."

His brother archdeacon, whose first visit to Athens it was, was quite overcome by the beauty of the Parthenon.

"But I am bound to say that I feel just a little guilty", he said, "when I think of the Elgin Marbles in the British Museum. Surely we ought to consider giving them back to their native place?"

Craggs, as usual, took a somewhat breezier view. "Most of them would have perished completely by this time if they'd been left here," he replied. "No, I think Lord Elgin did the world a good turn when he carried them off to England. Look how badly those statues on the Erechtheum have weathered! Besides, one could argue that any amount more people see them where they are. By the way, I see they're restoring the Parthenon; I wish one could feel sure it will look better when they've done with it! I suppose it's a shocking thing to say, but I often wonder whether places like Fountains and Rievaulx and Tintern can ever have looked half as beautiful in the days of their glory as they do now that they're in ruins. Oh, I know the moral's a bad one, but there it is! As we both know to our cost, well-meaning restorers can do quite as much harm as Vandals."

"There are some churches in my archdeaconry which have been utterly ruined by the piety of well-meaning people," said Castleton, with a sigh.

"The Gothic revival!" said the Archdeacon of Thorp.

"Encaustic tiles!" said the Archdeacon of Garminster.

"Early nineteenth-century glass!" chanted the one.

"Brass altar rails!" came the antiphonal response.

"Gilbert Scott!" cried Craggs.

"Poor dear Butterfield!" responded Castleton.

Both felt somewhat the better for having thus relieved their feelings.

"But my dear Castleton," said Craggs, "these are almost blasphemous thoughts for such a place on such a day as this. Come along, and let us restore our moral tone by looking into the Acropolis Museum: it's got some lovely things in it, I remember."

There both of them paid homage to the famous owl of Minerva, which induced in the Archdeacon of Garminster some speculations as to the reason why that particular bird had been selected to have such a reputation for wisdom.

"I could never bring myself to deny, with my long experience of clerical meetings", he remarked, "that there is a very great deal to be said for silence as an alternative to speech, but it is surely carrying that principle a little far if one is never to speak at all—for Tuwhit, Tuwhoo, which is the only remark which the owl ever makes, can hardly be regarded as a contribution to knowledge!"

"After all," said Craggs, "I believe the Romans had a god of Speaking Intelligibly who never made a single remark! It looks as if the ancients regarded the value of silence as a profound truth which they wished to lose no chance of inculcating."

"I remember a nice story in Herodotus," said his companion, "some people came to ask the Spartans for help, and knowing they disliked long speeches, only held out a bag, saying, 'The bag wants meal'; all they got by it was that the Spartans said, 'they had overdone it with the bag', which always seemed to me a little unkind."

"However, I'm prepared to admit that the owl doesn't *look* wise", said Craggs, "unless you're hypnotized by his stare—benevolent, yes, like this noble bird before us—but an owl-like countenance has never been regarded as particularly intelligent."

"Are you not forgetting Mr. Pickwick?" asked Castleton, "surely his face suggests a wise benevolence far superior to anything that mere intelligence can offer."

"True," replied Craggs, "though I seem to remember that Pickwick was sometimes loquacious; in fact, his very first appearance was in the role of orator."

"Ah, but how soon that role was dropped! Still, I confess that Mr. Pickwick was not like the owl which, as Gray tells us, 'moped' and 'complained to the moon': Pickwick never moped and very seldom complained, to the moon or anyone else."

"But we're wasting our precious time," said Craggs, "we mustn't linger too long even with the noblest of created owls. Let's ask Birtley about it to-night; he's sure to have some polysyllabic wisdom to impart to us."

With such discourse the pair entertained themselves as they strolled .round the Acropolis, but, as this chronicle makes no pretensions to be a guide-book, we will spare the reader any account of the further reflections which occurred to them there, or in the Athens Museum which they visited after lunch. That lunch, we grieve to record, was so meagre in its proportions and so unappetizing in its nature that Mr. Birtley, himself a Cambridge man, was moved to recall the undergraduate of an earlier generation who cried:

> "Think you that to a fool I've such affinity,
> As to consent to dine in Hall at Trinity?"

and his audience were moved to heartfelt sympathy by the lines which followed—lines which they felt singularly appropriate to the meal they were then consuming:

> "We still consume, with mingled rage and grief,
> Veal that is tottering on the verge of beef—
> Veal void of stuffing, widowed of its ham,
> Or the roast shoulder of an ancient ram!"

"I seem to remember," said Craggs, "that when Byron was coming back to Greece from Italy, his valet complained that they were returning to a land where all the wine was made of turpentine and all the mutton made of goat."

"Pretty true about the wine to this day," said Pycroft.

"The complaint about mutton is by no means peculiar to Greece," said Mr. Birtley: "there is a poem in which Godley envies those able to get to Switzerland to climb, and mentions among their blessings:
'They will dine on mule and marmot, and on mutton made of goats, They will taste the varied horrors of Helvetian table d'hôtes.'

" 'Athenian' would scan as well as Helvetian, and make equally good sense—but I see we are being bidden to betake ourselves to the Museum."

Sleuths in Athens

We have lingered, it is to be feared, too long over the æsthetic charms, and the gastronomic horrors, of Athens, and it is time to return to our more central theme, the political activities of Mr. Blades.

That evening, when the Wilsons, according to their custom, had withdrawn rather early to attend the ship's dance, the others gathered in a quiet corner of the smoking room to hear what Pycroft had to tell them of his inquiries at the British School.

"Quite interesting, as far as it went," he said. "There's no doubt that Shoe Lane chap is in with the Opposition—the Government's had its eye on him for some time, and there's also no doubt that the Opposition, or some of it, is hand in glove with the brigands: but that doesn't get us very far."

"As far as it goes, it rather suggests that Michalis was talking sense," said Craggs.

"Maybe, but you can't make much of a case against a man by saying that he knows a man who knows some people who are friendly with brigands!"

"Are the brigands really numerous still?" asked Castleton.

"Depends what you mean by numerous: there are quite a lot in the middle of Greece up in the mountains, and a certain number in the north part of the Peloponnesus. They bully the villagers, and no doubt they'd like to capture some travellers if they could—that'd suit them down to the ground, for the villagers are too poor to be worth robbing. The trouble is there aren't many travellers in those parts, anyhow not enough to keep a healthy brigand in the comfort he expects. It's a paying game if it comes off, of course, as it does once in a blue moon, but it's a bit dangerous. The Greek police can be bribed, and I fancy they pretty often are, but the Government doesn't at all want to have its tourists frightened away by a scare of brigands, so it's always to be reckoned with."

"Then you think there's nothing we can do about Blades?"

"Nothing so far, except keep an eye on the chap. Michalis may pick up some more. I think Mr. Castleton might as well tell him what we've learnt. I've written down the shopkeeper's name in case he knows anything about him."

Castleton took an opportunity of having another talk with Michalis and found that the shopkeeper's name was familiar to him as a man of very doubtful character.

"His *relations*, what you call his connections, are of the most detestable," he declared. "He is a man sufficiently rich, but the *provenance* of his riches—that one sees not! Assuredly it does not come from a little magazine—as you say shop—in Shoe Lane. No, no, Monsieur Castleton, as I have said to you, he inspires in me no confidence—not at all. This Blades, he is a man without honesty—that sees itself."

But in spite of the archdeacon's rather half-hearted plea that he should confide his suspicions about Blades to the captain's ear, Michalis obstinately refused to take any such step, repeating that that official would only mock himself of him.

"Gladly would I go," he said, "if I had of what to speak with certainty, but that, it lacks! The bricks, as you say in England, they make themselves not without the straw, and for the straw, it finds not itself!"

So matters remained during the rest of their stay in Athens, though Blades's absence from the moonlight visit to the Acropolis was the subject of unfavourable comment, if of no great surprise. There were those who believed that he had seized the opportunity of a nocturnal visit to his friend in Shoe Lane, but no one had been ready to forgo the Acropolis visit for the doubtful pleasures of sleuthing.

And so matters still stood when, a few days later, the wandering course of the *Lucretia* brought her to the famous island of Delos.

CHAPTER VIII

Disappearance on Delos

"He counted them at break of day—
And when the sun set, where were they?"
—BYRON

The peculiar fascination of islands is obvious, even to those who at times suffer from their limitations. Even the most ardent advocate of a Channel Tunnel, after he has successfully demolished all the practical objections—or has at least convinced himself of his success—still has to contend with a feeling, quite independent of reason, which tells him that, in spite of all he may say, Islands are Good Things, and that to be oneself an islander is a very glorious inheritance.

Few of us can hope, like the hero of Anthony Hope's *Phroso,* actually to possess an island, or to visit one, like Jim Hawkins in *Treasure Island*, in search of hidden wealth, but the appeal, to an Englishman, is both universal and undeniable.

For those who cannot expect to cruise, like Conrad, among the islands of the East Indies, or even to reach the Indies of the West, there is no better place than the Aegean in which to study islands in their native home, and the variety it offers is all that could be hoped for. You may find yourself on a spot made famous by deeds of arms in the last war, or by one renowned for fights of ancient days—you may find yourself greeted by the inhabitants with garlands and dances as the first of tourists to discover their existence. But, more commonly, if you are classically minded, you will be visiting an island once renowned in song, but now little more than a name on the pages of a Greek historian, or, if modern history be your subject, one which recalls to you the fact that it was the sailors of Greece, and in particular the islanders, who played perhaps the greatest part in the recovery of their country from the Turk.

Byron was quite right in singing the praises of the Isles of Greece, and, if he used perhaps a little poetic licence in saying that they lay in the sunshine of "eternal summer", there are certainly many days in the year when that compliment is well deserved: it was on such a morning that the good ship *Lucretia* found its way into the anchorage of Delos. Ever since, and undoubtedly before, the days of Shakespeare, the Englishman has had cause to lament with him that "full many a glorious morning" steals "unseen to West with his disgrace" of promise unfulfilled, and we have learnt to distrust that deceptive morning brightness which induces us to discard some of our clothing, or to leave our umbrellas behind. But the Greek sun seldom betrays the heart that trusts him, and this day was no exception to the rule.

The travellers had, as usual, received adequate intellectual preparation for their visit from Professor Tomkins, and his sad picture of the fall of that Athenian Empire of which Delos had once been the treasury had been a fitting introduction to a long quotation from The Vanity of Human Wishes: his performance deserved a kinder comment than that of Mr. Birtley that it was an admirable illustration of the Vanity of a (very human) Tomkins.

But neither tragic story nor cynical comment had had power to lower the spirits of the party, who were determined that no such reflections should mar their enjoyment of the day. Some looked forward to bathing in waters ampler than the *Lucretia*'s bathing pool could afford, and were by no means deterred by sinister rumours of the sharks which were said by some alarmists to infest the waters of the Aegean.

Disappearance on Delos

These stories had inspired Mr. Pycroft (who had served in the last war) with one of his unexpected reminiscences.

"You remember", said he, "how some of the less intelligent Americans used to say they'd won the war off their own bat? Well, there was a chap (an American himself) by the way—I shouldn't tell the story if he hadn't been, for I'm all for the Americans, even if they don't always quite appreciate all our virtues! But that's another story—anyhow, this chap wanted to get a bathe in a sea which was said to be full of sharks: he said he knew the way to get round them, and, in spite of all warnings, he went off and had his bathe. When he came back, they asked him how he'd got on and what this plan of his was—he said, 'Well, I got a bathing dress covered with the Stars and Stripes, and then I printed on it in large letters WE WON THE WAR, and I knew no shark would be fool enough to swallow that!'"

As they moved towards the shore, Craggs was reminded of what he called one of the best misprints he knew. It occurred in the description of some geologists landing to investigate an unknown island. "Imagine", it said, "our surprise to see lying on the beach a large number of erotic blacks!" Spooner could have told them that they meant "erratic blocks".

On Delos there are some admirable stone lions, and it is a great regret to the chronicler that neither of the events of the day took place in that setting, for it is one which he would have liked to describe, but truth is a stern master, and there is no denying that while one of these events took place on the shore, the locality of the second has not been precisely discovered to the present day.

For there were two events which marked, and slightly marred, their day in Delos, and one of them has a very definite bearing on the Story which we have to tell.

The first event was of a purely personal importance. Mr. Wilson, an enthusiastic bather, incautiously sat down on a sea-urchin, with results which made further sitting impossible for the moment and unpleasant for the future. He declared that it reminded him all too vividly of an interview with his head master some twenty years before.

The other event, though productive of less distress, caused considerable trouble to the ship's authorities. When the party returned in the evening, it was discovered that Mr. Blades's landing card had not been handed in, and a search of the ship revealed no trace of him. No one seemed to have seen him on the island, though he had certainly landed with the rest, and, though there were various surmises, such as that he had broken his leg scrambling up the rocks, or drowned himself while bathing, in neither case was there a shred of evidence to support the conjecture.

A party of volunteers made a hurried search of the island: the ship's departure was delayed as long as its time-table admitted, and a great deal longer than the captain would have wished. To keep to time was with him a point of honour, and to fail because of a tourist (one of a class which, as has been hinted, he held in small esteem) was to have insult added to injury. He confided to Craggs, who was rather an ally of his, that he would have borne it like a man if one or two others of the party had hurled themselves to destruction down the rocks. "That Lady Mary What's-her-name—she'd be no loss at all: I should be glad to see the last of her! But she stayed on the boat all day—what's she come on a cruise like this for, I should like to know, if she's too delicate to go ashore? But here she was, giving as much trouble as all the rest put together, complaining about everything and ordering all the stewards about—I tell you I was sorry for that companion of hers—a nice girl that! I could see she was ashamed of her: and this Blades too, I didn't know him but I gather he's no loss, though of course I shall have to account for him as if he'd been worth his weight in gold! Confound all pleasure cruises, that's what I say!"

Disappearance on Delos

However, despite the efforts that were made, no trace of Blades was to be found. The episode intrigued the passengers as much as it incensed the captain. No one was to be found who regretted Blades's disappearance, nor anyone who could claim more than the barest acquaintance with him: he had occasionally taken part in a game of deck-tennis but that had by no means added to his popularity.

"He was a surly sort of bloke and no fun to play with," was the verdict of one of the boys. "The worst of it was you couldn't trust him a yard."

It appeared that his interpretation of the rules had by no means been above suspicion, and deck-tennis, like fencing in old days, is one of those sports in which much is left to the honesty of the player. Since the affair in Crete, he had been left very much to himself, and had spent most of his time at the bar when it was open, or sleeping in a deck chair when it was not. He had never been known to attend a lecture, he had never been seen either on the Acropolis or at the Athens Museum, and on shore expeditions he had usually mooned away by himself.

"I think he must have known a bit of modern Greek," said another of the boys. "I remember seeing him jawing to some peasants, in Crete I rather think it was—yes, I remember now, it was that day when he got squiffy—and they seemed to understand one another all right."

His presence on the cruise was something of a mystery: there could be no doubt that he must have been duly proposed and seconded as a member of the Club, but the papers were naturally not available, and the secretary could not deny that it was physically possible for a signature to have been forged, or for the forgery to escape detection: the most he could say was that some members were sometimes perhaps a little careless in filling up forms without much inquiry, if they were asked to do so by anyone whose name they knew.

But it was far from obvious why a man of his character should wish to go on such a cruise at all: there were some of the passengers who were inclined to connect him with the purser's notice about possible thefts on board. But that official, when questioned, definitely declared that he had no evidence whatever to turn suspicion on Blades, still less any evidence on which a charge could be based.

Michalis made no attempt to conceal his delight at his disappearance.

"For me", he said, "there is nothing of which to grieve myself. I find myself disembarrassed of a companionship almost unendurable. Where he has gone, I know not, and I shall trouble myself of it not at all!"

To Archdeacon Castleton he confessed that he thought it possible that Blades had heard some news in Athens which made him anxious to conceal himself for a while. He had seemed somewhat anxious on their last night at the Piraeus. "But he was not of a type to make me the confidences."

"I believe", said Mr. Birtley, when they discussed the subject at dinner, "that it is now generally agreed that the criminal cast of countenance, as such, does not in fact exist. I myself have known several respectable, and indeed I may say eminent, ecclesiastics who displayed it to perfection. But Blades, it cannot be denied, afforded some support to those who maintain the theory: I have seldom encountered a more unprepossessing individual."

"Can't say I much liked his looks myself," said Pycroft. "He's not the sort that gets himself drowned."

The Archdeacon of Garminster was inclined to take a more charitable view, but even his charity could not maintain that Blades would be any loss to the party.

"I am sure", he added with a smile, "that Mr. Pycroft, as a good Yorkshireman, will not be content to regard him as a scion of the very respectable family of Blades of Sheffield!"

So there, for the time at least, the *affaire Blades* came to its inconclusive end. After long and sometimes acrimonious discussions between the captain and the officials of the Club, the *Lucretia* at last moved off, none too soon for the captain's equanimity. Her passengers were destined to meet further adventures, alike unfortunate and unforeseen.

CHAPTER IX

The Archdeacon at Bay

"Thou cam'st in such a questionable shape."
—SHAKESPEARE

From Delos the *Lucretia,* lightened of Mr. Blades, turned its head homewards round the south of Greece, of the headlands of which they enjoyed a distant view. Professor Tomkins seized the opportunity of explaining that the fortress of Monemvasia, situated on one of these headlands, and known as "the Gibraltar of Greece", had given its name to Malmsey wine, and excited some hilarity by giving a demonstration how, under the influence of that wine, a man, gradually becoming thicker and thicker in his pronunciation, could pass from one name to the other. One of his audience was heard to remark that even Blades himself could not have given a more convincing performance.

Cape Matapan, famous for its storms, did not, much to Mr. Craggs' satisfaction, live up to its evil reputation. On the contrary, he was able, as he looked at it from the deck, to recall some lines of Stevenson in which it figured: they appeared, he said, beneath a woodcut depicting a pirate with a long telescope lying on a precipitous mountain overlooking the sea:

The Archdeacon at Bay

Industrious pirate! see him sweep
The lonely bosom of the deep,
And daily the horizon scan
From Hatteras to Matapan:
Be sure, before that pirate's old,
He will have made a pot of gold,
And then he'll rest from all his labours
And live respected by his neighbours

MORAL: *You also scan your life's horizon*
For all that you can clap your eyes on!

"Stevenson had a very pretty taste in villains," observed Mr. Birtley. "There was that engaging ruffian in *The Wrecker,* whose motto was, 'Get hold of a rich man and make him squeal!' and I have always had a sneaking affection for that terrible little guttersnipe Huish, who appears in *The Ebb Tide.*"

"What about John Silver?" said Wilson.

"But remember the villainous hero of *The Master of Ballantrae!*" put in Castleton: "there was very little that was engaging about him."

"It's a nice word 'pirate'," said Birtley, going off on another tack. " 'Brigand's' a good name too—both better perhaps than the bearers deserve."

"I wonder if there really are many brigands in Greece nowadays," said Archdeacon Castleton, reverting to a question which had exercised his mind before.

"Pycroft seemed to think there were a goodish few," said Wilson, "but I'm afraid we aren't likely to meet any."

"I can't say that I particularly desire any first-hand acquaintance with them," remarked Mr. Birtley.

"Oh, how very unadventurous of you, Mr. Birtley," said Mrs. Wilson. "I think it would be delightfully exciting!"

"It certainly mightn't be at all uninteresting as an experience," said Craggs. "They might turn out to be the *Roi des Montagnes* type, which would certainly be good company."

"I am afraid", retorted Birtley, "that you are both viewing brigands through a haze of literary romanticism: I fancy that the Greek brigand (if indeed he exists at all) must be a singularly sordid specimen of humanity, with a very prosaic eye to plunder."

"Oh, how horrid of you," pouted Mrs. Wilson. "Now you've gone and shattered all my romantic dreams!"

"I wonder how many Greeks there are", said the Archdeacon of Garminster, "who can claim any sort of racial connection with the Greeks of classical times."

"Uncommonly few, I should think," said Craggs. "They've had a pretty desperate time, one way and another, and especially in this peninsula. But there's no denying they put up a very good show in their war of liberation in the last century."

"Pretty savage, I take it?" said Wilson.

"Oh, yes, they'd learnt that from the Turks, if they didn't know it already, but there's some very good fighting stuff in them."

"They rather like the English, don't they?"

"Yes, and on the whole we haven't done so badly by them—they've got a thrill for Lord Byron still: I'm told that, if you say you're a relation of his, there are still places where they'll give you a welcome."

"I have a friend", said Castleton, "who was a relation of Mr. Gladstone, and he found that if he mentioned the fact, he was very well received."

"The trouble is", remarked Craggs, "that it's uncommonly difficult for an Englishman to mention any fact at all in modern Greek! They've changed the grammar, and we've changed the pronunciation, and the result is that it's hard enough to read a Greek paper, and practically impossible to understand anything they say."

" 'Cigar's a useful word," said Pycroft.

"Cigar? How on earth do you use it? What does it mean?"

"It comes from σῖγα, which used to mean Silence, and it now means Go Slow: it's very useful to know it when your taxi-driver dashes down a hill, and I've found it come in useful when I was having my hair cut."

"Ever tried Esperanto?" asked Mr. Wilson.

"My dear Wilson", said Birtley, "I trust that no man of taste will ever be infected with that abominable disease! You may remember that Dr. Johnson said—I admit on questionable authority—to have said that the Scots had 'battened on the broken meats of human speech' to put their language together. That phrase exactly expresses my opinion of Esperanto. I should add that on the occasion in question Dr. Johnson is said to have just been told that he was in 'a bunker', so that his constitutional antipathy to the Scots had some particular justification."

Further along the deck, Mr. Michalis was engaged in an animated conversation with Mrs. Burslem. He had secured a high place in that lady's estimation by the praise which he had lavished on her purchases in Athens, which (to tell the truth) he privately regarded as both ugly and extravagant—but who can blame a courteous gentleman—and we know that Mr. Michalis was noted for his attention to the ladies—for encouraging one of the fair sex to believe that her taste was impeccable? or can claim never to have encouraged such an illusion himself?

He was now engaged in telling her of a friend of his who kept a shop in Olympia, which they were soon to visit—a shop little known save to connoisseurs. "It would give me a true pleasure, Madame", he was saying, "to present my friend to you, for he and you, you are both lovers of the beautiful. It is not that you should buy of him—that makes nothing—but that you should see and admire!"

"But if I see a good thing, Mr. Michalis, I want to buy it," said Mrs. Burslem. "There's no good me going there just to look!"

"Without doubt, my friend would see in Madame a person for whom he might part with some of his treasures: that arranges itself easily, is it not so? Me, I do not know, but if Madame permits, I will accompany her, and if she desires, I will do my possible."

"Well, that's very kind of you, Mr. Michalis, very kind, I'm sure," said Mrs. Burslem. "I just don't understand these shopkeepers who don't want to sell things. With my poor husband—he was in the drapery business in a very big way—35 big shops he had—it was just the other way—'Advertise! Advertise!' he used to say—'it's no use waiting for the customer to come to you—you've got to find him out and tell him just what he wants.' But I daresay things are different in a backward little country like this. I tell you, Mr. Michalis, I shall be real glad to find myself back in Manchester: we may not have all this sun there, but shops we do have, and sensible fixed prices without all this bargaining. I tell you it just drives me crazy never knowing from one day to another what those coins of theirs are worth."

Mr. Michalis murmured his sympathy and gratefully took his departure, having firmly promised to guide the lady to his friend's residence in Olympia.

Further still along the deck, Lady Mary was asleep, with her faithful companion sitting at her side. Miss Hillcroft, an attractive young lady of twenty-two, we have not so far had the opportunity of introducing formally to our readers for the simple reason that her attendance on Lady Mary left her with very little time for mixing in the social life of the ship. Nor could it be said that she found her ladyship a pleasant companion—or, rather, a pleasant person to be "companion" to. Lady Mary was entirely self-centred, and there were good reasons for the belief that her family had shipped her off to the Mediterranean in the hope of securing a month or two's peace and quiet; for her self-centredness was compatible with a consuming desire to interfere in the activities of others, and to put her relations generally to rights. They had smoothed the path, and overcome her objections, by offering to provide someone to look after her, as she declared that her delicate health made it unthinkable that she should travel alone, and had offered the post to Phyllis Hillcroft. She was the daughter of a small squire on whom, as a result of two sets of death duties, "poverty" (to use Isaac Walton's fine phrase) "had come like an armed man, and reduced him to a necessitous condition", so that she leapt at the chance of seeing Greece for nothing, and, in spite of all that she had to put up with, had never regretted her decision.

It would have been absurd to maintain that Miss Hillcroft was beautiful and at least equally absurd to deny that her looks were attractive. Her hair was black, with a blackness more Irish than Italian, and therefore more pleasing to a Northern taste: her eyes were grey: and if purists complained that her nose was her worst feature, there were others who felt that its slight tilt showed character.

At the moment she was engaged in a hasty study of *Baedeker*, so as to be able to make the most of the visit to Olympia.

Lady Mary opened a sleepy eye.

"I really don't think that I shall feel up to landin' tomorrow," she said, "these expeditions are so very tirin'. I think we had better have a quiet day on the ship when everyone has gone. That will be much more restful."

Phyllis could hardly conceal her dismay at the idea.

"Oh, I was so looking forward to seeing Olympia," she said. "There seems to be such a lot to be seen there, and I was hoping you would enjoy it too."

"You *must* learn to think more of other people," said Lady Mary. "You know how easily I get knocked up: how could I enjoy it if I had one of my dreadful headaches? The doctor particularly said that I was on no account to get overtired."

Phyllis Hillcroft realized that it was an occasion for guile. "Of course, I quite understand," she said. "You mustn't dream of going if you don't feel up to it. But I'm afraid poor Professor Tomkins will be dreadfully disappointed: he was telling me only yesterday how much he was looking forward to showing you the Hermes and hearing what you thought of it."

This crafty approach to the subject was not without effect.

"He ought to know what a strain it is on me," said her ladyship. "People are so dreadfully inconsiderate! I think you ought to have told him you knew I wasn't up to it. But, as you seem to have led him to expect it, I will see what I can do. But it would mean that I must keep very quiet to-day. What a tiresome noise those people make walkin' round the deck! I wish you would ask them to be more quiet. Let them walk, if they must, though I must say I find it very disturbin', but surely they needn't keep on talkin'."

Phyllis, well satisfied with her partial success, promised to do her best to abate the nuisance, and Lady Mary composed herself to slumber again.

Mrs. Wilson was one of those young ladies who are commonly described as "arch". Archness is a quality difficult to define, and perhaps its nature depends rather on the temperament of those on whom it is exercised. Our two archdeacons, though differing from one another in many respects, were agreed in disliking it, and saw with alarm, on descending to dinner, that the lady was unmistakably in one of her arch moods. She wagged her finger reproachfully at Archdeacon Castleton as he took his seat.

"You are a very naughty man!" she cried. "How could you try and keep us in the dark? I do think it was too unkind of you. Here are you letting us all think you were just an ordinary clergyman, and all the time you were a Venerable Archdeacon. Aren't you ashamed of yourself?"

She appealed to the company for support. Castleton, with a hurried glance at Craggs, made the best defence he could.

"So the horrid secret is out!" he said. "May I ask how you penetrated to the truth?"

"I had a letter from my mother, which ought to have been given me in Athens, but it got mislaid, and I only got it given me to-day. She says she's heard from a Miss Wolsingham who lives in Garminster—she was at school with her years ago—and she says—let me see, what does she say?" She unfolded the letter— "Yes, here it is! 'Do tell your daughter to look out for our Archdeacon who will be on her boat—his name is Castleton; I am sure she will like him, though'… oh, perhaps I'd better not read the rest!"

"Oh, please go on," said Castleton, "I am well accustomed to being criticized by Miss Wolsingham, who keeps us all up to the mark in Garminster!"

"All right then!: 'though his kindness of heart often makes him close his eye to the follies of the clergy whom he is supposed to keep in order.' "

"I am glad it is no worse," said Castleton, smiling. "Miss Wolsingham is always having mild quarrels with her vicar. He is a very good fellow, but he is unwilling to let her have her own way entirely, and that is what she really wants!"

"But you haven't answered my question," persisted Mrs. Wilson. "Why have you kept us in the dark all this time? Think of all the reflected glory we should have got from having a real live archdeacon at our table!"

"I am afraid", said Castleton, "that you greatly overrate the distinction! Archdeacons are by no means so glorious as you suggest: in fact there was a time when their reputation was decidedly low."

"Wasn't there some old wheeze about it being impossible for an archdeacon to be saved?" asked Mr. Wilson. "I seem to have heard one."

"It was not so much a statement as a question propounded for discussion," said Mr. Birtley, "and it was put in a very unflattering way—*Num Archidiaconus salvari possit*?"

"You know I can't understand your horrid old Latin," said Mrs. Wilson, petulantly. "Do explain what it means!"

"The Latins", said Birtley, "had two ways of introducing a question: if they said *Num* it expected the answer No: if they said *Nonne* it expected the answer Yes, as the Latin Grammars used to say. Consequently, in this case, the answer expected was one unfavourable to the prospects of archdeacons at the Day of Judgement."

"How horrid of them! Why was that?"

"They were financial authorities, responsible for keeping the clergy up to the mark, and there was a suspicion that they were in the habit of feathering their own nests."

"Oh, dear," said Mrs. Wilson, "I don't think I like you after all, Mr. Castleton! Archdeacon Castleton, I mean. Are you as horrid as that nowadays?"

"I hope not," said the Archdeacon of Garminster, with a smile: "but in any case it was only the clergy who had any grievance. So you and Mr. Wilson would have been quite safe from us."

"Well, I've had a little lesson in Latin grammar anyhow," said Mrs. Wilson, rising. "Come on, Jack, let's go and dance!"

"A deplorably arch young lady," said Castleton, with a sigh.

"The use of the word 'arch' is curious," remarked Mr. Birtley. "I believe it is explained in the Oxford Dictionary as meaning 'innocently roguish'—fortunately the word is not in very common use, or the public might come to expect 'innocent roguery' from archbishops, while you yourself would suggest an 'innocently roguish deacon'—a very horrid thought!"

"She's more roguish than innocent, I fancy," said Craggs, gloomily, to Castleton, as they left the saloon. "I only hope she won't find me out next!"

"Oh, I think you are safe enough: she will hardly have time to get any more letters, even if Miss Wolsingham, or someone like her, should happen to write to her about you. I think that you may reasonably hope to continue to pass as plain John Craggs for the rest of the voyage."

The hope, reasonable as it appeared, was, as we shall see, not destined to be fulfilled, though no one could have foreseen the circumstances in which it was to be dramatically shattered.

CHAPTER X

Games at Olympia

"And take away his train."
—SHAKESPEARE

The competitors at the Olympic Games, and the spectators, arrived, it is to be supposed, by land: if any arrangements existed for those who came by sea, they have long since disappeared; in any case, the small harbour of Phea provided no accommodation for a vessel of the size of the *Lucretia*. She had to lie at some distance from the shore, and a longish journey in the ship's boats had to be faced by the passengers: in calm weather this was by no means unpleasant, but when, as on this occasion, there was a stiffish breeze, the choppiness of the passage was extreme. One of the boats was indeed driven out of its course, and reached the shore some time after the others.

In this boat, as ill luck would have it, was the unfortunate Archdeacon of Thorp, who found himself repeating, on a small and ignominious scale, his experience of the Bay of Biscay. Another of its passengers was Lady Mary Culham, who had at the last moment yielded to the importunities of Professor Tomkins, adroitly organized by Miss Hillcroft. Her ladyship, though (or perhaps because) she was an excellent sailor herself, had no sympathy with those who suffered from seasickness, and did not fail to remark on the inconvenience to which their selfishness exposed others. She regarded Craggs's misery with unfeigned disgust, and even remarked audibly on the inconsiderate behaviour of bad sailors in refusing to remain on dry land.

But at last the harbour was reached, and the passengers boarded one of the smallest and absurdest trains in the world. As it was by no means full, the hapless archdeacon was able to secure a carriage in which he could lie at full length and might hope to recover tone.

The train pottered slowly along the valley, giving the passengers ample opportunity of studying the ugliness of the vine in its earlier stages—"so like the human race", as Mr. Birtley, a bachelor, observed. Professor Tomkins seized the opportunity of explaining to his carriage-full the nature and value of the currant crop which takes its name from Corinth: he refused rather sulkily to discuss the question, raised by one of the junior members of the party, whether, in the case of sultanas, the fruit gave the name to the lady or the lady to the fruit.

It was hot, dry, dusty and gusty when they finally reached Olympia, and as they made their way to the Museum, Mr. Birtley was heard to remark that, whatever might be justly said against those who desired the palm without the dust, it was eminently reasonable to deprecate having the dust without the palm.

The Hermes in the Museum received his inevitable tribute of admiration, and most of the company dispersed to eat their picnic lunches in comfort in a spot commanding a good view of the racecourse. When luncheon was over, the more earnest seekers after truth followed the Professor in a minute survey of its arrangements. Foremost among those who accompanied him, ostensibly as disciple but more obviously as critic, was Miss

Bustard, whose appearance recalled that other Cambridge lady so mercilessly described by J. K. Stephen: of her, as of that other, it might have been truly said that:

> *She had such a hat*
> *As neither merits nor expects remark:*

But it would have been a gross slander to continue the quotation and to say that:

> *If she thought of anything, it was*
> *That So & So had got a second class*
> *Or Mrs. So & So a second child.*

Miss Bustard thought a great deal, and on very intelligent subjects; it is true that, secure herself in the possession of a First Class in the Classical Tripos, she may occasionally have allowed her mind to dwell, whether in pity or contempt, on the inferior achievements of others, but she was a whole-hearted lover of the classics, and devoted much of her thought to proving that the Professor was not quite as omniscient as he believed himself to be. She had made no secret of her regret that the *Lucretia*'s usual lecturer had been unable to make the trip.

Miss Hillcroft, having left Lady Mary to all appearance soundly asleep, felt at liberty to follow the Professor's party at a distance, though keeping a watchful eye on her slumbering employer. The Major and Mr. Ryland were among those over whom Tomkins exercised an almost hypnotic influence, and they followed obediently in his train. The Wilsons had gone off on an expedition of their own: Pycroft had disappeared, while Birtley had persuaded Castleton to come back to the Museum for a closer examination of the Hermes, whose merits he regarded as grossly exaggerated. They had tried to persuade Craggs to accompany them, but the train journey, a very shaky affair, had done him but little good, and the hot sunshine had definitely done him harm. He said that he felt a second dose of the Museum would be the finishing touch, and decided to lie down under the shade of some trees in the hope that a little sleep would revive him.

Meanwhile, Mr. Michalis was fulfilling his promise to introduce Mrs. Burslem to his friend the shopkeeper, and had found her far from unwilling to desert her more classically minded companions.

"Call that a racecourse!" she said, contemptuously. "It's clear the men who laid that out had never been to Aintree. By the way, Mr. Michalis", she went on, "I thought I saw your friend, Mr. Blades, just outside the station. You didn't see him, did you?"

Michalis gave a sardonic laugh.

"Blades! No, Madame. I saw him not nor do I wish to see him of my life. Nor is it to me that he would seek to introduce himself. But that he should be here at all, assuredly it is all that there is of least possible. Look you, that he should make the escape in Delos, that explains itself, but that he should come here where there are those who know him, that, pardon me, Madame, I find it a thing unbelievable."

"Oh, well, it was someone like him," said Mrs. Burslem, unconcernedly.

The shop, in the variety of its goods, proved worthy of all that Michalis had said in its praise, though whether the particular objects displayed were worth the price suggested for them is perhaps a somewhat more debatable question. But price, as we know, was a matter of indifference to the lady, and bargains were concluded to mutual satisfaction, after prolonged inspection and a torrent of eloquence from the shopkeeper.

When all the chaffering was over, he insisted on entertaining his patroness to a cup of Turkish coffee, which took an unexpectedly long time to prepare, and, by the time it had been ceremoniously consumed and some more compliments exchanged, a glance at his watch showed Michalis that it was high time for them to start for the station if they were to catch the train. He apologized for hurrying Mrs. Burslem, and after final salutations they set off together.

By the time they reached the station the train was already showing signs of irritable impatience, and Michalis was only just in time to hurry her into the last coach, which was fortunately empty.

Another even later arrival was Lady Mary Culham. She and Phyllis Hillcroft had set off in good time, but when they had got rather more than half-way she discovered that she had left her purse behind her, presumably in the place where she had been enjoying her nap. Blaming Phyllis bitterly for her carelessness, she sent her back to fetch it, declaring that she would not move a step further until it was retrieved.

This took some time, and, as it was impossible to convince her ladyship that the train would not wait for a person of her eminence, the rest of the journey was accomplished at a dignified pace: they also just found a place in the last coach as the final whistle blew.

At the very last moment came two other still more belated passengers. Mrs. Wilson had got tired of walking and had sent her husband off by himself, saying that she would join the Professor's party and come back to the train with it. But his eloquence soon palled on her: she drifted off by herself, sat down on a grassy bank and fell asleep: when she awoke, she was horrified to find that everyone else seemed to have gone, and set off vaguely to run after them. But a sense of direction was not her strong point: she lost her way, and anything might have happened either to her or to the Archdeacon of Thorp, whose slumbers had been even more profound, had she not happened to stumble on him as he lay dreaming under his friendly tree. He awoke refreshed, and was able to guide her: even so, it was only by very hard running that they were able to jump into the train when it was already in motion.

Mr. Wilson, meanwhile, assuming that his wife was with the Tomkins party, as she had said she would be, was peacefully ensconced in the forward part of the train: only at the last moment had he felt any anxiety about her, and that was removed when, putting his head out of the window, he witnessed her tardy but triumphant arrival.

"By Jove! That was a close-run thing!" he said, sinking back into his seat. "I was a fool not to begin worrying about her before, but, as it is, it's lucky I didn't: all's well that ends well!"

In the last coach there was by no means so much complacency. Lady Mary was deeply insulted at having been made to hurry, and reminded Miss Hillcroft that hurrying was one of the things which her doctor had expressly warned her to avoid. She contrasted the care and consideration which she had seen Michalis showing to Mrs. Burslem with the failures of Phyllis.

"I have no doubt it was he who had the train kept back," she said. "If it had not been for him, we might have missed it altogether. How often I have tried to impress on you the importance of punctuality!"

Mrs. Burslem was equally loud in his praise.

"I call him a very attractive young man," she said. "He took me to a very nice shop—very expensive some of the things were, but I never mind paying a good price when one's buying a good thing. As my poor dear husband used to say, 'it's quality that tells', and that was how he built up his business: there's hardly a man in Manchester to-day who isn't wearing Burslem braces—and I've always made it my motto. I shall look forward, Lady Mary, to showing you some of the little things I've bought: I know you will enjoy seeing them."

Lady Mary, whose dislike of Mrs. Burslem had been steadily

growing, and who regarded the mention of braces as indelicate in the extreme, responded with what in a person of less aristocratic extraction would have been a grunt: if there was one thing which annoyed her more than another, it was to see things bought by other people which she could by no means afford to buy herself, and to have to admire Mrs. Burslem's "bargains" would be the final straw.

"But where *is* Mr. Michalis?" asked Mrs. Burslem. "I thought he was getting into the carriage with me: I do hope he hasn't been left behind."

"I expect he got into one of the other carriages in this coach," said Craggs, who had by this time recovered his breath: "they all seemed pretty empty from the glimpse I got of them."

"I am afraid we shall be terribly jolted in this last coach," complained Lady Mary. "Don't you remember, Phyllis, that I specially told you we ought to make sure of a carriage in the middle of the train? I very much dislike bein' shaken, and I know it is very bad for me."

"I am afraid we none of us had much choice, Lady Mary," said Craggs, anxious to defend Miss Hillcroft from blame which was clearly undeserved. "Anyhow, the jolting seems to be getting less: I wonder why we are going so slow."

"What else can you expect on a potty little line like this?" said Mrs. Burslem. "Why I do declare we're stopping!"

The archdeacon put his head out of the window. "Good heavens," he cried. "They've slipped this coach off."

The others, except Lady Mary (whose opinion of Craggs had been extremely low since his culpable surrender to seasickness) hastened to the window on either side.

There was no doubt of it.

At this point the line turned a corner, round which the front part of the train had already disappeared: the last coach lay marooned on the line, a strange and lonely object in the midst of the vineyard which offered a somewhat uninteresting foreground on either side: behind them the hills rose up to north and south of the valley.

"How extremely provokin'!" said Lady Mary. "If we had started soon enough, Phyllis, we should have been in the front part."

"Jack will have no idea what's become of me," lamented Mrs. Wilson. "I'm afraid he'll be dreadfully upset."

"That comes of those bad couplings," said Mrs. Burslem, who seemed disposed to take the situation more philosophically—"now if they'd only employed an English firm, this sort of thing couldn't have happened."

"They're bound to find out soon and come back for us," said Craggs, "till then I'm afraid there's nothing to be done."

"I can't bear to think what Jack will be feeling," wailed Mrs. Wilson, dissolving into tears.

"This carriage is dreadfully uncomfortable," said Lady Mary. "I do wish, Phyllis, that you had remembered to bring that second cushion—it would have made all the difference."

"We shall be terribly late for dinner," said Mrs. Burslem.

These various *motifs* dominated the lamentations which occupied the next half-hour with an unpleasing monotony; their only effect was to force a bond of sympathy between Phyllis Hillcroft and the Archdeacon of Thorp, neither of whom joined in the chorus.

At one moment hopes were entertained that the resourceful Michalis would arrive to their support, but, as time went on, it became only too clear that he must have been left behind in Olympia. As no other protesting heads appeared, it became clear that their carriage was the only one in the coach to be occupied.

At the end of half an hour, the silence which had surrounded the stranded coach was broken by a noise of voices: Craggs went to the nearest window and looked out: at the same moment a head appeared at the opposite side of the carriage: it presented the unattractive features of Mr. Blades.

CHAPTER XI

The Journey

"I travelled among unknown men."
—Wordsworth

"Get out!" said Mr. Blades.

Lady Mary, besides being a little deaf, was so delighted at the prospect of succour from the outside world that she disregarded this unceremonious approach and welcomed him with effusion.

"Oh, Mr. Blades!" she said, "How very kind of you to come to our help! We were just beginning to wonder whether——"

"Get out!" repeated Mr. Blades, opening the carriage door as he spoke.

Lady Mary was speechless, but there seemed nothing else to be done: she began to descend, followed by the other ladies.

"What's all this about, Blades?" cried Craggs, over their heads.

"You'll see soon enough," was the laconic response.

Blades motioned to them to pass round the back of the coach: there they found half a dozen ruffianly looking Greeks sheltering from the sun: two of them were armed with antiquated rifles, and the rest with murderous looking knives in their belts.

"Look here, what's the meaning of this?" asked Craggs again.

The only answer which Blades vouchsafed was to give some orders in Greek, as a result of which his companions surrounded the party.

"You can't do this sort of thing!" protested Craggs, and the ladies united their voices with his, Mrs. Burslem's accents being particularly strident.

The Journey

"Can't I?" said Blades, and he motioned to the escort to move on.

Resistance was clearly impossible: Blades led the way round the coach again on a narrow track through the field of vines towards the north. There was nothing for it but to follow, shepherded as they were by their unwelcome escort. To Craggs's expostulations and the questions of the others no answer whatever was given. On the other side of the vine field, they found a country lane; in it, two mules were waiting in charge of two more Greeks, at least as villainous in appearance as the rest. Blades turned to Lady Mary.

"Get up, you," he said rudely, signing at the same time to Mrs. Burslem to mount the other mule. "The rest of you'll have to walk."

This was too much for Lady Mary's self-control: she broke into hysterical screaming, from which it was to be learnt that her doctor had strictly forbidden any violent exercise, that she had not ridden since she was a girl, and then of course on a side saddle, and finally that the British Government would assuredly avenge such an outrage on a well-known member of the aristocracy. All was of no avail: she was hoisted, none too gently, on to the back of the leading mule, and lay there feebly moaning.

Mrs. Burslem, warned by her fate, made no attempt at active resistance, though, if her captors had understood the very forcible remarks which she addressed to them, they would certainly have treated her more roughly still. Phyllis went to the support of her employer and shored her up unsteadily on the off-side.

The archdeacon was in a very awkward position. Boiling with rage at Blades's insolence, he was sorely tempted to knock him down and, as he had some knowledge of the Noble Art, might very possibly have succeeded, but the odds against him were too heavy. Had he been alone, he would certainly have made a bolt for it, and might conceivably have got away, but being the only male of the party he clearly could not desert his companions. There was nothing to be done except to stay where he was and wait upon events.

At length the party moved off towards the mountains on the north, the mules going first, with a man at each of their heads and Miss Hillcroft at the side of Lady Mary's animal: Blades followed with a couple more of his band, and the rest brought up the rear, after Mrs. Wilson and Craggs, who walked together. She had pulled herself together in spite of her distress about Jack.

"I suppose they *are* brigands?" she said to the Archdeacon.

"Not a doubt of it, I'm afraid. I wonder how that brute Blades comes in: we knew he'd some connection with them, but I never thought it was as close as this. I'll try to get something out of him a bit later on, and see if I can find out where he's taking us to."

After an hour or so's walking, mostly uphill, he made the attempt, but met with no success. Blades scarcely condescended to open his mouth, and the most that he could be induced to say was that he was taking them to the boss, and that they would have to wait till they saw him.

"Not much to be got out of the sulky brute," said Craggs, falling back to join Mrs. Wilson. "Oh, there was one other thing. I asked him how long we should have to walk, and he said we shouldn't get there before night: I only hope you're a good walker."

"I expect I can keep on going", said she, "for a few hours anyhow: it's lucky that dancing keeps one in pretty good training, but I hope they'll give us a bit of a rest before long."

They trudged on in silence for a time, and were soon beginning to descend into what looked like another valley parallel with that from which they had climbed.

The Journey

"There's just one bit of good luck", said Mrs. Wilson—"or may be. I mean Michalis getting left behind. I don't see how he can possibly have got into the front part of the train, so he must have stopped in Olympia, and as soon as he hears what's happened he may be able to do something—they must have rung up from the other end: he's so clever, he'll be sure to know what ought to be done."

Craggs, who had completely forgotten all about Michalis, welcomed the idea.

"Yes, he's a very capable chap, and as he's a Greek himself, he'll know the ropes—that's certainly a good idea."

Both of them stepped out more briskly for this encouraging thought, and, their road being downhill, they made good progress for a little. When they reached the little river, a brief halt was allowed, and they were able to wash and refresh themselves with a cooling drink from its waters.

Lady Mary was by this time in a state of resentful coma and Mrs. Wilson kindly suggested that when they set off again she should take Miss Hillcroft's place at the mule's side—a change which her ladyship would certainly have resented had she been in a condition to notice it. Mrs. Burslem was full of not unreasonable complaints of the discomfort of her saddle and the perversity of her mount, but the party as a whole were too tired to indulge in any coherent discussion of their position or their prospects.

All too soon they were bidden to set off again, their path this time winding upwards, and growing steeper and steeper.

"Pholoe, I believe this mountain's called," said Craggs to Miss Hillcroft, who was now walking by his side, "or it may be Erymantus—I know those are the ranges to the north. I hope we haven't got to get to the top of either of them."

Miss Hillcroft responded suitably, and they fell into a pleasant conversation, trying to keep their thoughts away from the dangers and difficulties before them.

"I've got a confession to make," said Phyllis, after a while. "The truth is, I've always known you were the Archdeacon of Thorp."

"The deuce you have!" cried Craggs. "You don't mean you were the lady who wrote——"

He broke off suddenly, for he found it quite impossible to believe that she could have been the author of that sentimental letter about the secret which the two of them shared.

"I never *wrote* anything," said Phyllis, "but I did try to ask your advice once."

A light broke in on the archdeacon.

"Oh, so you were the lady on the deck, were you?"

"Yes, I was—and then, just when I was going to tell you about it, we were interrupted, and when I tried the next night, it was somebody else, and I'm afraid I was so rattled that I ran away without saying anything."

"I'm so sorry," said Craggs, "I seem to have been very stupid. Do forgive me. There are two things I want to know now: first, how you came to know me, and then what it was you were going to ask me about?"

"The first is quite simple: you know the Thornleys, don't you? Well, Sir Thomas is an old friend of my father, and I was staying with them once, about two years ago, when you came over to inquire into some row in the parish. You wouldn't remember me, of course—there's no reason why you should—but I knew you again the moment I saw you. I didn't say anything about it, because I realized you didn't want to be recognized, and of course I never told anyone."

The archdeacon was delighted at her consideration and said as much, apologizing at the same time for his own forgetfulness.

"Now for the second question," he said. "What was it that you wanted to consult me about? I seem to have done very poorly all round."

"Well, I expect it was very silly of me, but I simply didn't know what to do. One morning I'd got an hour off, and I thought I'd go and have a little sleep in the sun, so I climbed into one of the boats on the top deck, which I believe is strictly forbidden, and there I went fast asleep. I was wakened by two people talking just underneath: I couldn't hear much and naturally I didn't want to, but I did hear something about jewels, and I heard them say 'in a safe'—so I got it into my head that they might be planning some robbery on the ship. Of course I've no idea who either of them was."

"One was Blades, for a fiver," interjected the archdeacon.

"I expect so, but I didn't think particularly about him then: I barely knew him by sight. Well, as I say, I simply didn't know what I ought to do. I didn't want to go to the purser, partly because it was just suspicion, and partly because I didn't want to say I'd been asleep in a boat—I knew what Lady Mary would think about that, and so I thought I'd ask you for advice. But it didn't come off very well," she ended ruefully.

"I'm afraid that was all my fault," said the archdeacon, and he explained how it came about that she had encountered a different archdeacon at the second attempt.

"Not that you need have been afraid of Castleton," he said, "he's the mildest of men, and would have given you much better advice than I could—but you couldn't very well have known that."

This exchange of confidences not only beguiled the way but increased their esteem for one another, and by the time a second halt was reached, not until darkness was coming on, their intimacy was appreciably advanced.

As Blades had foretold, night was falling by the time they arrived at what was apparently their final destination. It was a cave near the top of a steep little mountain, the path to which the mules negotiated with some difficulty, while the walkers found it a severe scramble. There the ladies were unceremoniously bundled into a cave, of which the only amenities appeared to be some sheepskin rugs which promised warmth and at least the possibility of sleep. Lady Mary declared, indeed, that sleep would be impossible, but those who had witnessed her achievements in that line on a hard chair at a lecture on the *Lucretia* took a more sanguine view of her prospects. Both she and Mrs. Burslem appealed to the archdeacon to tell them what was likely to happen next, but he could only reply that he would talk things over with them in the morning, and they were both too tired to insist on a discussion at the moment. As Phyllis was following into the cave, she drew Craggs aside:

"There's just one thing I've picked up which you might like to know: I believe this mountain is called Lasion, or something like that: I heard one of the men talking on the other side of the mule as we began to climb, and he seemed to say that two or three times and pointed to it. He didn't know I was listening, and I don't suppose it matters, but I thought you might like to know. Good night."

And she vanished into the cave.

The archdeacon was left alone. Seeing Blades near by, he went up to him and demanded where he was to sleep. Blades jerked his hand towards a small recess in the rock a little way off.

"You'll find a sheepskin in there. The boss wants to see you in the morning. No monkey tricks, mind!"

With that, he turned on his heel.

Craggs investigated the den allotted to him, and decided that, tired as he was, he would have a pipe before turning in. There was a small terrace running between the caves, and he paced up and down smoking, conscious that two or three of the guards kept a watchful eye on his movements.

As he paced along, he saw a figure emerge from the ladies' cave, and for a moment hoped that it might be Phyllis Hillcroft, possibly bringing some more information: in any case, he did not conceal from himself that another talk with her would not be unpleasant.

But the voice which addressed him was that of Mrs. Wilson.

"Oh, Mr. Craggs," she said, "I've got a confession to make to you!"

"What, another of them!" thought the disappointed archdeacon, and for an instant his mind played with the thought that she might be followed in her turn by Mrs. Burslem and Lady Mary, each with a load upon her conscience and a need for spiritual counsel.

"Really, Mrs. Wilson?" he said, pulling himself together. "Now what can that be?"

"I didn't feel I could go to sleep until I'd told you," said Mrs. Wilson, whose fatigue had evidently wrought some havoc with her nerves. "It was so dreadfully stupid of me, and somehow I feel as if all this was a kind of judgment for it. And so rude, too," she added, showing a slight tendency to whimper.

"Oh, come, Mrs. Wilson, I'm sure it can't be as bad as all that. Just pull yourself together and tell me all about it."

"It was I who wrote that letter," gulped Mrs. Wilson.

"What letter do you mean?"

"The one about the s-s-secret b-between us!"

"Oh, you mustn't bother about that," said Craggs, realizing what she meant. "I'm sure you only meant it as a joke—but tell me how it happened, if you like,"

Mrs. Wilson was slowly regaining confidence.

"You see", she said, "I found out that Mr. Castleton was the Archdeacon of Garminster. I really got that letter from my mother long ago, and then I thought it would be rather fun to tell him that someone *did* know it. So I wrote that letter and made Jack put it under the door. He wanted me to put 'All is discovered: fly at once', but I thought that would be silly, and then I began chaffing

The Journey

him at breakfast, and you said it was a letter from an old friend of yours, and Jack and I were so amused."

Mrs. Wilson giggled somewhat hysterically at the retrospect.

"Then it wasn't meant for me at all?" asked the Archdeacon of Thorp, a little resentfully.

"For you? Oh, no, of course not. How could it be? You haven't got a guilty secret too, have you?"

"No, no, of course not!" said Craggs hastily, blushing a little under cover of the darkness. "Now, my dear Mrs. Wilson, you really mustn't worry any more about it. I will explain it all to Archdeacon Castleton, and I can promise you he's the very last man to feel any grievance. You must go and get as much sleep as you can. I'm afraid we have a rather strenuous day before us."

Mrs. Wilson withdrew, comforted, to her cave, and Craggs resumed his solitary pacing. So there were two mysteries explained, creditably, in the one case, and comprehensibly, at least, in the other. How very like the arch Mrs. Wilson to play a silly trick like that! On the other hand, there was no denying that Miss Hillcroft came out of it very well and had had terribly bad luck. A nice girl that, and uncommonly sensible. What shocking luck for her to be tied to an old absurdity like Lady Mary!

His pipe ended, he retired to his primitive resting place, wrapped himself in his sheepskin, and composed himself to slumber. It was not long before sleep came to him, after his fatiguing day. Night and silence settled down on Mt. Lasion—if Lasion was indeed the mountain's name.

CHAPTER XII

An Anxious Interlude

"How were they lost?"
—Shakespeare

Leaving the unfortunate captives to enjoy what sleep they may, we must return for a brief period to the remaining members of the Hellenic Travellers' party.

On the arrival of the train, after a slow and tedious journey, the accident to the last coach was of course discovered, and immediate steps were taken to find out what had happened to its unfortunate occupants. No alarm was felt, and almost all the party were taken off at once to the ship, but a few remained behind to welcome the involuntary truants on their return.

Of these Mr. Wilson was naturally one, and Castleton stayed too, partly from a charitable desire to keep him company, and partly because he felt that Craggs would be glad to see him there. Pycroft announced his intention of staying also, for his residence in Greece had left him sceptical of the efficiency of the Greek railway authorities, and he felt that his slight knowledge of modern Greek might prove of some use.

It was not until nearly two hours had passed that any definite information came through, and when it did it was by no means satisfactory. All that could be said was that the coach was standing on the line, but that there was nothing whatever to show what had become of its occupants. There were no houses within a mile or two of the place where it was stranded, and the fields near by—as indeed they had noticed for themselves from the carriage windows—were entirely devoid of human occupants.

For the first time, some real anxiety began to be felt, and the word 'brigand' began to pass from lip to lip. Wilson, the person most closely concerned, was in a pitiable state of alarm, and the others could think of nothing reassuring to suggest to him. All that they could do, with the help of the ship's representative, who had stayed to give any assistance he could, was to insist that the local police should be mobilized at once, and this demand was only conceded after a strenuous denial that such a thing as brigandage was conceivable in so well ordered a district.

Pycroft was far from satisfied.

"I don't believe they, any of them, mean to do a thing," he said. "Anyone could see that that inspector, or whatever he was, is a perfect fool—besides, I doubt if he's really got much authority. I'll tell you what I'll do—I'll see if I can get on to my friend in Athens, and ask if he can put the wind up them there: they won't at all want an international scandal."

It was not till after long delay that at a very late hour he succeeded in getting his call through. His friend, who had had to be called out of bed to take it, was at first far from enthusiastic, but as the story was unfolded his interest grew, and he promised to see what he could do, even offering in the end to go round and see the British Minister himself. As that dignitary was known to like keeping very late hours, this generous suggestion was warmly welcomed, and the three departed feeling that at any rate they had done everything in their power.

The officer in charge of the boat which took them off took a gloomy view of the situation.

"I don't like to think what the Old Man will say about it," he remarked, "and I only hope he won't say it to me. He was in a fearful rage about losing all that time at Delos, and I expect he'll be nearly frantic now: there'll be a regular set-to between him and the secretary of the Club; all I know is I shall do my level best to keep out of his way for a bit."

"It does comfort me a little to think that they have Michalis with them," said the archdeacon to Wilson, who was in the depths of depression. "He is such a very competent fellow, and his knowledge of the country and of the language will be of great use to them."

But Wilson refused to be comforted.

"These wops and dagoes haven't any idea how to run a search even if they wanted to, and, if you ask me, I believe in their hearts they're all on the side of the brigands. Pycroft says that policeman chap was a fool: I'm much more inclined to think he's a knave, as likely as not standing in with the brutes himself."

No one could deny the possibility, and it was in very gloomy mood that they crept to their cabins at a very late, or rather a very early, hour, hoping that the coming day would bring some better news.

But it did not, and in fact brought no news at all, except that the Greek Government, as a result of the representations of the British Minister, were sending some soldiers to supplement, or perhaps to stimulate, the exertions of the police.

"They don't look up to much," said Wilson, when he saw them.

"There's one good thing about them anyhow," said Pycroft. "Metaxas may be all that his enemies say, though I think myself he's a lot better than they make out, but there's no doubt he's a strong man, and he certainly holds no brief for brigands, who are by way of being the spoilt children of the Opposition. I think his troops will play up all right."

"The worst of it is not having any idea in what direction they've taken them," said Wilson. "No one seems to think one direction's more likely than another. That's what makes me feel sure there's some hanky-panky about the business: don't tell me the natives here haven't a very shrewd idea which is the right way to look—

An Anxious Interlude

but as far as I can see, there's no way of making them say."

"It is difficult for us", said Birtley, "to be quite fair to the Greeks: I fancy that, if we ourselves had been ruled by the Turks for a few hundred years, our national virtues (such as they are) might have become somewhat obliterated—but I quite see that that's very little consolation to you."

The situation as it stood when another day had passed is not unfairly set out in the following quotation from the London Press:

"BRIGANDAGE IN GREECE?
Titled Lady a Captive.

Our Athens correspondent cables:

Six British subjects have disappeared in circumstances which give rise to the fear that they may have been captured by brigands. As a party of the Hellenic Travellers' Club was returning by train from Olympia, the last coach became disconnected, in circumstances which have not yet been explained. When the accident was discovered, investigations showed the coach standing empty on the line, and no information as to the passengers was forthcoming. The local police and the authorities in Athens were at once informed, and a search was at once instituted. It is reported that some troops have been sent to the district. In official Greek circles the idea of brigandage is scouted, and it is expected that the missing tourists will soon be discovered.

The names of those missing are given as follows:
Four ladies: Lady Mary Culham, Mrs. Burslem of Manchester, Mrs. Wilson of Ross-on-Wye, Miss Phyllis Hillcroft; and two gentlemen: Mr. J. Craggs and Mr. Michalis—the latter of whom is of Greek extraction.
The S.S. *Lucretia*, in which they were travelling, is lying off the port of Phea, awaiting the results of the search."

Gloom reigned on the *Lucretia*—deepest perhaps in the captain's cabin, though there it was from time to time illumined

An Anxious Interlude

by fiery flashes of anger: in the intervals of acrimonious interviews with the official representatives of the Club, the captain occupied himself in cursing his officers, his crew, his passengers, the Greek police, and, above all, the evil fate which had condemned him to conduct an adjectival pleasure cruise.

It reigned unrelieved throughout the quarters of the passengers, though slightly alleviated for the younger members of the party by the ghoulish pleasure which they took in exchanging anecdotes as to the horrible outrages perpetrated by Greek brigands in the past. There even came to Miss Bustard's ears the scheme of a complicated sweepstake as to which portion of which missing passenger's anatomy would accompany the first demand for ransom. When she found a young lady who had drawn Lady Mary's ear offering to sell it for half-a-crown, and a young gentleman proposing to exchange Mrs. Burslem's little toe for Mr. Craggs's little finger, she felt it was time to make a stand, and, with the help of Mr. Ryland and the Major, stifled the scheme before it came to the ears of Professor Tomkins, to whom the shock might well have proved fatal.

But, even so, Rumour continued to flap her ugly wings, and nerves were distinctly on edge. A well-meant offer by the Professor to occupy their minds by a lecture on the Inner Meaning of Greek Tragedy was considered by many of the passengers to be in doubtful taste, and he withdrew it in some dudgeon.

Of the victims, it was perhaps Mrs. Wilson and Mr. Michalis whose fate caused the most general concern: both of them were well known and well liked, and the obvious distress of her husband aroused general sympathy: few professed to have much personal feeling for either Lady Mary or Mrs. Burslem, and Phyllis Hillcroft and Craggs, though highly esteemed by those who knew them, had for different reasons moved in a somewhat narrow circle. But there was no one who denied that it was a very bad

An Anxious Interlude

business from every point of view, and sympathy for the victims was reinforced in some breasts by a dislike of having their plans upset, and by the inevitable uncertainty as to when they would be able to get home.

They lay, as Mr. Birtley was not slow to observe:

> *as idle as a painted ship*
> *Upon a painted ocean,*

each with his own particular albatross suspended round his neck, and could realize to the full the inconvenience of such an appendage.

But it is time for us to go ashore again, and to return to our involuntary cave-dwellers.

CHAPTER XIII

The Brigand Chief

"It may seem strange to find his manners bland."
—BYRON—*DON JUAN*

The early sun shone brightly into Craggs's cave, revealing, had he been in the mood to enjoy it, an extremely beautiful view. Not long afterwards, a disreputable brigand made his appearance, bearing a chunk of bread and a flask of wine, and before very long Blades arrived with a message to say that "the boss" was ready to receive visitors.

Craggs followed him, full of excitement, round an angle of the mountain top, and was ushered into a cave somewhat more elaborately furnished than the others, though its furniture consisted only of a couple of low divans, and a few good rugs on the floor. At the far end of the cave was a curtain, apparently screening off a further recess.

The archdeacon stood for a few moments looking out on the view, which on this side was glorious enough to divert his thoughts: his contemplation of it was interrupted by a voice which seemed strangely familiar.

"Good morning, Mr. Craggs," it said.

He turned and saw standing just before the curtain the figure of Michalis, but a Michalis strangely transformed: he was wearing a shooting jacket of good cut, and his whole attire was that of a sporting country gentleman.

"Good Lord!" gasped Craggs. "You don't mean to say *that* *you're* the brigand chief!"

"Oh, didn't you guess it? That is more than I dared to hope! It's really most gratifying!"

The archdeacon's brain was in a whirl.

"So you can talk English all right," he said, inconsequently, uttering the first thought that came into his head.

Michalis laughed heartily.

"Why, of course I can!" he said. "So you didn't guess that either? Better and better. But do sit down and let us talk comfortably. Yes, I can't tell you what a relief it is not to have to go on jabbering in Anglo-French," he went on, motioning Craggs to a place on one of the divans, and taking his seat on the other. "You see, the trouble is that I really know very little French, so that I had to keep on using the same elementary idioms over and over again: I really think someone ought to have spotted that," he added, shaking his head reproachfully.

"But look here, Michalis——"

"Perhaps I ought to explain that Michalis isn't my real name either. But it's not a bad name, do you think? You see, in Greece, it's nearly as common as Jones is in England, so there's the least possible risk of getting other people into trouble."

The archdeacon felt that this conversation, interesting as it was, was getting them nowhere, and that he must make an effort to bring Michalis to the point.

"Well, what do you expect to get out of us?" he asked. "I don't suppose you brought us up here simply to admire this very remarkable view."

"It *is* a good view, isn't it?" said Michalis. "I'm so glad you like it. Do you know, I really feel that I owe you something of an apology. But do have a cigarette, won't you? Do you mind their being Turkish? or perhaps you'd prefer your pipe? I'm afraid I've only Greek tobacco, and I can't say I can honestly recommend that."

He proffered a box of cigarettes as he spoke, and gave Craggs a light.

"You see, the fact is", he went on, "I know that when people say 'the fact is' it almost always means they're lying, but I can assure that it's not so in this case—the fact is that I didn't want you here at all: it was all a careless mistake."

"A very uncomfortable mistake for us!" said Craggs grimly.

"Yes, I'm afraid so, and I'm really very sorry about it,' said Michalis, "and that reminds me," he went on, becoming more and more the perfect host, "I am afraid you may not have been able to shave this morning. It's so tiresome, isn't it? for dark-haired people like ourselves not to be able to miss a single day without its becoming so painfully obvious." He passed his hand, as he spoke, over his beautifully shaven jaw, making Craggs uncomfortably conscious of his own bristles. "Do remind me, when we've had our little talk, to send you round my razor: I'll tell one of these fellows to bring you some hot water."

"That will be extremely kind of you," said Craggs, sarcastically, "but I think you were saying something about its all being a mistake."

"Yes, a mistake of that stupid fellow Blades. It really is extremely tiresome not to be able to see to things oneself: one has to employ the best agents one can get, and sometimes (as I should have said on the *Lucretia*) they are of a stupidity unbelievable! Now Blades, within his limits, is a very capable fellow: his get-away from Delos was really quite well managed, don't you think? It was important to have him on the spot in time to get things going, and I'm bound to say that most of the work was very well done—and then, at the last moment, he goes and makes a perfect fool of himself."

Michalis paused and paid the tribute of a sigh to the scarcity of real competence in the human race.

"How do you mean 'made a perfect fool of himself'?" asked Craggs, interested in spite of himself.

"Why, you see, the only person I really wanted captured was Mrs. Burslem. As no doubt you've noticed, she has quite an indecent amount of very valuable jewellery, which she habitually wears. It was lucky for me, by the way, that she refused to take any notice of the purser's warning. I expect that was due to some indiscretion of Blades. I really must teach him to be more careful, but you know how difficult it is with uneducated fellows like that! You'd hardly believe it, but I caught him prowling round Mrs. Burslem's cabin—in Wilbraham's dressing-gown, if you please; the fellow's no brains at all!"

Michalis sighed again, with a silent appeal for sympathy. "However, the first part went well enough," he went on, "though, as a matter of fact, he seems to have showed himself very incautiously at the station. But the railway officials were most helpful, and the uncoupling of the carriage couldn't have been better done. Where Blades fell down, was in allowing all you people to get into that last coach."

"I don't quite see how he was to help that," said Craggs, finding himself absurdly impelled to take part in this ridiculous conversation.

"Oh, surely!" said Michalis, a little pained at his slowness of comprehension. "All he had to do was to tell the stationmaster, a most reliable fellow, to wave all late arrivals on to the coaches ahead. But he forgot to do it, and so there we are!"

"Here we are, indeed," echoed Craggs, "and I very much wish we weren't."

"I do see your point of view, I do indeed," said Michalis earnestly, "but you mustn't speak as if all the difficulties were on your side. It meant that I had to provide another mule at great inconvenience—there really are very few mules available just now. I should have liked to get some for the other ladies, but it simply couldn't be done. I do hope they weren't terribly tired?"

"It was a stiffish walk for them," said the archdeacon.

"Yes, I'm afraid so: I've had some coffee made and taken round to them: they must have a good rest to-day. And that brings me to another point," he continued, "just to show you that all the trouble isn't on one side; these unexpected guests have thrown my catering arrangements completely out of gear—it's so difficult anyhow to keep good servants in these days, and I don't like to think what my cook will say! But he'll do his best, I'm sure."

Craggs was getting thoroughly tired of this airy persiflage.

"Do come to the point," he said sharply, "What is it you want to get out of us?"

"I was just trying to explain," said Michalis, plaintively, "you really must let me put it in my own way. After all, we've plenty of time before us, haven't we? Well then, Mrs. Burslem, as I was saying, has a great deal of very valuable jewellery, that I was anxious to secure."

"To steal, you mean?"

"I do wish you wouldn't be so hasty! Mrs. Burslem is a wealthy woman, to whom the loss will be insignificant. Besides that, I have good reason to believe that she is heavily insured. If she parts with her jewels, no one will be appreciably the worse off, and I shall be appreciably the gainer. I am interested, Mr. Craggs, in many good causes in Greece, which in a poor country like this are badly in need of support. I hardly feel that, if you think the matter over, you can blame me for wishing to benefit them at the expense of a trifling loss to a few shareholders in a prosperous insurance company."

"Then you yourself stand to make nothing out of it?" asked the archdeacon, incredulously.

"I shall be content with the satisfaction of having done my country a service," replied Michalis, looking him straight in the face.

Craggs frankly did not know whether to believe him or not: he spoke like an honest man, but he had already considerable reason to distrust appearances where Michalis was concerned: in any case, there was no way of disproving his assertions.

"Then if Mrs. Burslem surrenders her jewels, the rest of us can go, can we?" he asked.

"Certainly, subject of course to certain inevitable charges: you would hardly believe how 'overheads' mount up in a business like this. Labour is cheap in Greece, certainly, but even here you would be surprised to learn how much it costs to hire and equip a dozen brigands, and even then they're a rough lot. I hope they behaved properly yesterday?"

"So far as I could judge," replied Craggs, sardonically, "they carried out their instructions with reasonable efficiency."

"Good, I'm delighted to hear it! I hope I may tell them you said so: some of them are quite pathetically anxious to please.

"One or two of them," he went on, handing his cigarette-case to Craggs, and taking another cigarette himself, "are very keen to learn English. That young chap with a bandage on his arm, Dmitri—I don't know if you noticed him? He picked up quite a lot from a rich American we had up here for a few weeks. But his accent is very transatlantic, and I should like

The Brigand Chief

him to get some teaching. Such a nice young fellow—he's a bank clerk in ordinary life, and has a widowed mother to look after: and there's another, Spiro, who's very anxious to learn too."

"Don't their parents mind their going off like this?" Craggs felt impelled to ask: Michalis certainly created a moral atmosphere of his own.

"Oh, no, they think a few days in the mountains will be very good for them—it's terribly stuffy down there in the valley—and the bank officials are very reasonable. Poor Spiro's brother had an unfortunate accident last year: one of the police shot him by mistake—that's really very rare, though they will not teach them to handle their rifles carefully: he was really doing very well with me—still he gets a pension all right, as it was an accident in the course of his employment."

"But to come back to the point," said Craggs, afraid he might have to listen to biographies of all the band. "What was the charge you were thinking of suggesting?"

"Ah, yes, you must forgive me. I know I'm sometimes rather a bore about my young fellows: it's like running a Scout troop, and one gets very fond of them. What I had in mind was £100 a head: that would work out at about £30 a night, for I hope you won't be here more than three days, but there would be no extra charge if you decided to stay the whole week: I hope that doesn't strike you as unreasonable?"

Craggs, who was himself a man of some means, was privately a little relieved to hear that no more was demanded, but he felt bound to make a protest.

"It seems to me pretty steep," he said, "for the accommodation is decidedly primitive."

"Ah, but think of the view," said Michalis. "There are very few hotels in Europe which can offer you anything to compare with that!"

"Can't you make a reduction for a party?" asked the archdeacon, entering into the spirit of the thing, as it seemed hopeless to induce Michalis to take it with more gravity.

"I considered that very seriously," said Michalis, "and if you had been a family, I think it might have been done, but to do it for what I am afraid I must call a scratch party would be very difficult. You will realize that it might establish an inconvenient precedent."

Craggs pressed the point that Miss Hillcroft, being in attendance on Lady Mary, was in a somewhat different position, and after some discussion Michalis, who showed every desire to be reasonable, consented to halve her contribution.

Encouraged by this success, Craggs raised another point. "You said £30 a night," he said. "That'd be £90, not £100."

"We are forced to make a charge of 10 per cent for attendance," replied Michalis gravely: "we find it saves so much inconvenience to our visitors in the matter of tipping."

"But that only brings it to £99," objected Craggs.

"Ah, the extra pound is for table money," said Michalis, without moving a muscle of his countenance.

"But there aren't any tables!"

"No, but it's the principle of the thing—besides, it includes dancing: we find a really inclusive charge is so much more popular. But now, if that is settled, Mr. Craggs, perhaps you will be good enough to let the ladies know what we have arranged. If they agree, and I am sure I can rely on you to put the matter clearly before them, I shall ask you to write a letter to one of your friends on the boat—I would suggest Mr. Castleton, but that is a point I leave entirely to you—telling him the facts, and I will enclose a line saying exactly how the payment is to be made. That shall be sent off with the least possible delay, and I have every hope the little matter can be cleared up within 48 hours."

There was nothing more to be said, and they parted; Michalis again expressing his hope that the archdeacon would not take amiss his confession that he had not been an expected guest.

"It sounds so rude", he said, "when one puts it like that, but I can truly say that it has given me great pleasure to make your better acquaintance, so, selfishly, I can't regret it. I have much enjoyed our little talk: it is such a comfort to meet anyone to whom one can talk quite freely."

When the archdeacon returned to the ladies' cave he found the situation extremely strained. Lady Mary, who, to all outward appearances, had passed a very peaceful night, was fully persuaded that she had hardly closed her eyes, and resented bitterly the suggestion that her snoring had deprived Mrs. Burslem of sleep. Mrs. Wilson, when appealed to by both sides, gave her verdict in favour of the lady from Manchester, and Lady Mary's temper grew worse and worse. She relieved it by abusing Phyllis Hillcroft, whom she had come, by some obscure process of reasoning, to regard as primarily responsible for the situation in which they found themselves. This palpable injustice roused the other two ladies in her defence, and language became heated.

Another grievance was the long absence of Mr. Craggs, which her ladyship resented as a sign of disloyalty. Mrs. Burslem contented herself with saying that, if it had been dear Mr. Michalis, he would certainly not have left them so long alone; but Lady Mary, so far from welcoming this qualified support, took the opportunity of saying that it was a great pity that the Hellenic Travellers' Club did not take more care to ensure the good breeding of its members: she did not know Mr. Michalis herself, she said, but his low origin was apparent, nor could she understand the pleasure which some people seemed to take in his company. As these remarks were accompanied by a meaning glance at Mrs. Burslem, fuel was added to the flames, and that lady suggested that it was rather the high and mighty airs which some people gave themselves (though she would name no names) which marred the harmony of life on the *Lucretia*.

So, on the whole, Mr. Craggs did not return any too soon. But the news which he brought did nothing to restore harmony. When he told them that it was Michalis who was responsible for their captivity, Mrs. Burslem flatly refused to believe it, and her arguments in his favour led to the acid comment from Lady Mary that it took the eye of a gentleman or a lady to distinguish sheep from goats in the social sphere. She reminded the company of the views which she had herself recently expressed.

Nor did the situation improve when he explained the reasons which had led to their capture. Lady Mary's wrath was instantly concentrated on Mrs. Burslem as the cause of all their trouble, and she expressed herself with a vigour which belied her claims to be a frail invalid.

She spoke of vulgar ostentation and purse-proud arrogance with an eloquence worthy of a puritan reformer, and it was necessary for Phyllis and Mrs. Wilson to restrain Mrs. Burslem from resorting to physical violence.

But worse still was to come. When it became known that the innocent victims of a mistake were not, as they at first fondly hoped, to escape scot-free, then indeed was "Satan's invisible world displayed", and it became manifest that, however sensitive Lady Mary might be in other respects, to touch her purse was to touch her in the most tender spot of all.

After not obscurely hinting that Craggs was himself in league with their captors, she roundly declared that she could not, and would not, produce £100 or anything like it, and, when reminded that the alternative was to remain indefinitely in the hands of the brigands, dissolved into hysterical collapse: the names of the Prime Minister, her nephew the Duke, and the King himself were occasionally distinguishable in her frantic outbursts. At last she relapsed into the silence of exhaustion, and Craggs was able to turn to the other members of the party, while Phyllis gave such first aid as circumstances allowed.

Mrs. Burslem and Mrs. Wilson raised no difficulties about the payment, though the former lady, at last convinced, ceased not to execrate the perfidy of Mr. Michalis. "To think that he was fooling me all the time," she cried, "and I dare-say those things he made me buy weren't nearly worth what he got me to pay for them! and then I had to leave them all in the train."

"I believe I saw one of the men carrying them up, Mrs. Burslem," put in Mrs. Wilson.

"Well, that only makes it worse! He'll only steal the lot of them. I can't think what my poor dear husband would have thought of me. Often and often he's given me a warning. 'Never, Emma,' he used to say, 'never do you buy things without a guarantee: get a written guarantee and you're safe—' but what's the good of that with a lot of rascally Greeks who, as like as not, can't even sign their own names? There's only one good thing about it—those jewels of mine that they took last night, they're all insured, and well insured too, though I say it myself. I don't hold with coming into these foreign places without making sure you won't lose by their thieving ways. I daresay, when all's said and done, I shan't be any the poorer after all. 'If you insure, insure for a bit more than the thing's worth', Mr. Burslem used to say, and that I've done, and thankful I am for it."

Mrs. Wilson treated the matter more lightly still. "Of course I'll pay," she said. "I hate being done like this, by a skunk like that, but it's no good squealing about it, and it might have been much worse. I'm not going to pretend that £100 will ruin me. All I want to do is to get out of here as soon as I can, so the sooner you write that letter, the better I shall be pleased."

All seemed to be going well, but a further and even uglier storm arose when the archdeacon disclosed the arrangements made about Miss Hillcroft.

The Brigand Chief

"I'm very sorry, Mr. Craggs," said Phyllis, "but I simply can't ask my people to stump up £50. They just haven't got it. As I was telling you last night, my father's been absolutely ruined by death duties, and he and my mother are only living in a corner of the house. I wouldn't have dreamt of this trip at all if it had been going to cost them anything."

"I was assuming that, as you were Lady Mary's companion, she would feel responsible for you," said Craggs, lowering his voice.

It had appeared that Lady Mary was past thought or speech, but the suggestion of any further financial responsibility roused her with startling rapidity.

In a flood of voluble invective, she declared that nothing would induce her to pay a penny for Phyllis, whose carelessness she again denounced as a prime cause of all their disasters. If anyone was to pay for her (which seemed in itself unreasonable) she maintained that it ought clearly to be Mrs. Burslem, who was, if possible, even more directly to blame.

There is little doubt that Mrs. Burslem, who was by nature a kind-hearted woman, would have been perfectly ready to produce £50 if the suggestion had come from a different quarter, or been urged in a different way: as it was, she flatly refused to do anything to help Lady Mary to shirk her obvious responsibility, remarking that no real lady would have suggested such a thing. Craggs and Mrs. Wilson, both outraged by this display of selfishness, declared in chorus that they would be delighted to make themselves responsible for the money, Mrs. Wilson remarking in a whisper that she quite understood Mrs. Burslem's point of view.

A document was accordingly drawn up, by which the sum of £450 was jointly and severally guaranteed, and Craggs departed to compose the letter to be submitted to Michalis's critical eye. He took considerable pains over the composition of his letter, for he knew that it would be subjected to very close scrutiny:

however at last it was completed, and he took the two documents along to Michalis's cave. As he had expected, his letter was read with much care, and it was with a sigh of relief that he heard that it had passed muster. Michalis said that he would type it out at once, and while he was doing so he handed to the archdeacon a copy of the instructions which were to be sent with it. With them he, in his turn, had no fault to find.

The typing completed, Michalis invited him to affix his signature.

"I'm very glad things are so comfortably settled," he said. "I will send them down at once by the most trustworthy of these young ruffians: I'm afraid he may find it difficult to deliver them till night, for it wouldn't do for him to be caught—but he's not without a certain shrewdness, and I think he can be trusted to get it through. If so, I shall hope for an answer to-morrow.

"Now I wonder what we can do to amuse you? I'm afraid we can't let you go very far, and you'll have to be followed by a guard, but the view, as you know, is well worth looking at, and there's a rough track round the mountain top."

Craggs thanked him, and said he would ask the others.

"By the way, may I ask what the name of this mountain is?" he inquired.

"Oh, I don't think there's any harm in your knowing, now that everything is so happily arranged: it's called Mt. Lasion—it's really an offshoot of the Pholoe range. I'm sorry I haven't got a map to offer you; that always makes the country so much more interesting, doesn't it? But I'm afraid I haven't any up here. I've a few novels, by the way, in case any of you want something to read, and a little poetry: I find the newer poets extremely interesting, though I confess my own tastes are all conservative. Some of T. S. Eliot I can manage, but some of his later verse seems to me very difficult—and as for Ezra Pound!—but I mustn't keep you talking."

He ushered Craggs out of the cave with the utmost politeness: on his return he found the ladies sitting in a somewhat gloomy silence.

Mrs. Wilson said she would much enjoy a stroll, and Phyllis showed an unmistakable desire to accompany her, but Lady Mary declared that she could not possibly be left alone. Mrs. Burslem, who was too stiff to walk, said she would sit outside in the sun, with an obvious desire to avoid her ladyship's company: she asked Craggs to get her a book, and he took a somewhat malicious pleasure in providing her with a volume of Ezra Pound, while selecting for Phyllis a detective story from Michalis's library, its owner frankly confessing that the detection of crime had for him a peculiar fascination.

The archdeacon, who had been privately hoping for a stroll with Phyllis, contented himself with Mrs. Wilson's company, and was bound to confess that in a situation of real difficulty her archness vanished, and she revealed herself as both sensible and good-natured.

The day was slow in passing, and an account of its hours would be as tedious to read as they were to endure: they went early to rest, not without hope that their next day of captivity would also prove to be their last.

CHAPTER XIV

The Letter

"Though I beheld at first with blank surprise."
—Wordsworth

The Archdeacon of Garminster had retired early to bed: the continued absence of news and the anxiety were beginning to wear

The Letter

him down, and he had no heart for the conversation of the smoking room, where tempers were beginning to get frayed by unending speculation, futile suggestions of action, and indiscriminate criticism of "the authorities" for getting nothing done.

He undressed slowly and sadly in his lonely cabin. The process was nearly completed when he heard footsteps outside: a steward knocked, entered and handed him a letter.

"This has just come for you, sir," he said: "No one seems quite to know how it got here, but it was found lying on the deck."

Castleton took it and opened it: his excitement was so obvious that the steward waited in the doorway.

"Will there be any answer, sir?" he asked—though it was far from obvious how he would have proposed to deliver one.

"What's that? No—no—or wait a moment, steward! Will you kindly ask Mr. Pycroft, Mr. Birtley and Mr. Wilson to meet me at once in the smoking room? Please tell them it's most important and that I hope they will come as soon as they possibly can."

"Yes, sir. What shall I do if the gentlemen are in bed, sir?"

"That makes no difference. Tell them that I very much want to see them as soon as possible."

"Very good, sir!"

Castleton huddled on a few clothes and made his way to the smoking room: there he found Pycroft and Birtley already awaiting him and Wilson was not long in joining them.

The room was fortunately deserted, for bridge, like dancing, being considered somewhat indecorous at such a time of anxiety, the lecture which Professor Tomkins had provided on Thirty Centuries of Mediterranean History had proved unexpectedly popular.

Castleton took them into a corner.

"I am sorry to have been so urgent with you," he said apologetically, "but I have just had a letter from Craggs."

The Letter

"From Craggs?" cried Wilson. "How are they all? How's Mary?" The others were equally excited.

"Told the captain?" asked Pycroft.

"No, it only came five minutes ago, and I thought I should like to show it to you first, as there is nothing which can be done tonight. Here it is: I'd better read it to you.

'My dear Archdeacon,

We are all safe, but prisoners: here are the terms for our freedom: £100 to be paid for each of us, and £50 for Miss Hillcroft—£450 in all. I have advised all our party to accept, and they have all agreed to do so, though Mrs. Wilson says she cannot agree without her husband's authority. Please tell him that *the question emphatically expects the answer Yes*. I cannot tell you where we are, of course; all I can say is that we were all lame and nearly blind when we got here. I need say no more. Please make all arrangements: the enclosed paper contains full instructions as to the method of payment.

Yours very sincerely,

J. B. S. CRAGGS.'"

"Well, thank heaven they're safe!" exclaimed Wilson. "But Mary must have gone dotty—I can't think what in the world she means by saying she's got to ask me: she's got plenty of money of her own and can spend it just as she likes. She can't imagine I shouldn't want her to."

"It *is* a comfort to have heard at last," said the archdeacon. "I do hope they have not been ill treated."

"They seem to have had a bit of a job getting up to wherever they are," said Wilson. "The sun was pretty blinding that day, I remember."

"I imagine there is nothing to do except to take it to the captain," said Castleton. "No doubt he and the purser will know how to arrange about the money side of it. I am afraid I am not

The Letter

nearly as competent as I ought to be. I am a little surprised that poor Craggs should have fixed on me as the right person. Of course I will gladly do anything I can, but I shall have to depend on the help of others. Perhaps you will be good enough to advise me, Mr. Pycroft?"

"Certainly—glad to do anything I can. Mind if I have a look at the letter?"

"Of course not, here it is."

Pycroft read the letter in silence.

"Anything strike any of you about that letter?" he asked.

"What exactly do you mean?" asked the archdeacon.

"Nothing in particular: I just wanted to know how it struck you: you might read it again."

The others gathered round and read it together.

"Well?" said Pycroft. "Anything strike you, Castleton?"

"No, I don't think so—except that it seemed to me a little curious that Craggs should seem to take it so easily. Of course one knows nothing of the circumstances, and I need hardly say that I am not reflecting on him in any way, but I should have fancied, from my short acquaintance with him, that he would have expressed himself rather differently. Oh, yes, there is one other thing: it surprises me that he should address me as Archdeacon: he has never called me by that title, and, as you know, it was a little joke between us to try to keep it secret. That is all, I think, except, as I said, that I thought it strange he should entrust the business side of things to me—but no doubt he intended that as a compliment."

"What about you, Wilson?"

"As I said just now, I can't imagine what made Mary send me that absurd message: she's got more money than I have, as a matter of fact, and there's nothing on earth to prevent her from writing a cheque for £100 if she wants to. It's just silly: I think Craggs must have misunderstood what she said."

The Letter

"He is a singularly accurate man," murmured his brother archdeacon, "at least that is his reputation."

"What about you, Birtley?" asked Pycroft.

"I must confess", answered Birtley, "that, from a purely literary point of view, it strikes me as rather a curious composition, suffering from a strange verbosity which I should not myself have associated with Craggs. But I gather that you have some special object in these inquiries? May I ask what it is?"

"Well, I think it's fishy myself," said Pycroft.

"Will you elucidate that statement?"

"I'll tell you what I think—of course you may not agree. Take the points one by one: none of them at all important, but they do mount up. Point one—he writes to Castleton to do a difficult bit of business, though he knows (forgive me, Castleton!) that business isn't his strong suit. Point two—he addresses him as Archdeacon, which, I gather, is rather unexpected. Point three: he sends a message from Mrs. Wilson which her husband calls absurd, and none of us think him the sort of chap to make absurd mistakes. Point four—as Birtley says, the letter's written in a queer style. I know nothing about his ordinary style, but I should have expected him to express his meaning clearly."

"That is certainly his reputation," agreed Archdeacon Castleton. "I have heard him held up as a model to other clerical writers."

"The queer thing about the style", said Birtley, "is that sentence in the middle about 'the answer to the question': that's 'jargon', as Quiller Couch used to call it, and I should have thought Craggs was the last man to use 'jargon.'"

"Of course one must remember", protested the archdeacon, "that the letter was probably written under difficulties, and that he had to be very careful what he said."

"I can conceive no circumstances less likely to induce a man to write verbose jargon," remarked Mr. Birtley, with some acidity.

"That sentence about 'expecting the answer Yes' is the sort of thing one would never tolerate in a boy's essay."

The archdeacon had been studying the letter again. "There is another very small point," he said, "but as you are asking for small points, perhaps I ought to mention it. He usually signs himself 'John Craggs': I happen to know that, because he had some papers sent after him, and he asked me to witness his signature. Here, as you see, he signs himself 'J. B. S. Craggs'."

"We'll call that Point Five," said Pycroft: "All I say is that five queer points in a short letter is too many, and that taken together they do mount up."

Wilson was beginning to get interested. "I don't quite get the idea," he said. "Do you mean it may be a cryptogram or something?"

"I don't mean anything so definite as that, but I do think it would be worth while for us to look at it carefully again and see if any of these points suggest anything to any of us. You read them out, Birtley: I don't want you to think it's my private show."

The others agreed, and Birtley took the letter. "The first point was his calling you Archdeacon. I am bound to say that I see no particular significance in that." None of the others could make any suggestion, so, agreeing to keep it in mind, they passed on to the second point. "That was the point concerning Mrs. Wilson, wasn't it? I understand that you think she would have seen no necessity for any reference to you?"

"Not a chance of it. Mary's completely independent, in every sense of the word: she'd rather enjoy doing a thing like this all on her own, and only telling me about it afterwards. She's the last person in the world to talk about 'her husband's authority'—she never will allow I've got any! It's a regular joke between us."

"Could it perhaps", put in the archdeacon tentatively, "be intended as a jocular reference to that fact?"

"That's possible, I suppose."

The Letter

"It's hardly likely Craggs would want to put a family joke into a business letter," said Pycroft. "It looks to me as if, for some reason, he wanted to force Wilson, or Mrs. Wilson, into the front of the picture, so to speak, as she's the only person mentioned—and apparently mentioned with no real reason at all."

"Perhaps we had better pass on to Point Three," said Birtley. "Let me read the sentence, 'Please tell him' (that is, Wilson) 'that the question emphatically expects the answer Yes', and you will notice that it is underlined."

"That makes it even sillier than before," said Wilson. "There's no conceivable reason for her making such a fuss about it."

"I am more interested in the form of the sentence," said Birtley: "'expects the answer Yes' conjures up memories of the Latin grammar in my mind."

"Yes, don't you remember," cried Wilson, "you were giving Mary a lecture about it in that argument we had at dinner? I don't think you were there, Pycroft—you were dining at some other table—about *Num* and *Nonne*, I mean? '*Num* expects the answer No: *Nonne* expects the answer Yes': Craggs must have had that in his head."

"But what was the argument about?" asked Pycroft.

"I remember very well," said Castleton, with a smile. "Mrs. Wilson rather wickedly reminded us of the old question about the salvability of archdeacons, which was put in the form which expected the negative answer. *Num Archidiaconus salvari possit*?"

"And he says the answer is emphatically Yes," said Pycroft, meditatively. "I still don't see it. If you were the prisoner, Castleton, it would make sense. 'Can an archdeacon be saved, or rescued'? answer, 'emphatically Yes'—but, as it's not you but Craggs——"

"But he *is* an archdeacon!" cried Castleton, excitedly. "He is the Archdeacon of Thorp, I quite forgot you did not know." He hastily explained to the others their mild conspiracy of silence, and how, even after he had himself been detected, Craggs decided to maintain his incognito.

"It begins to look as if we might be getting somewhere," said Pycroft. "Here's an archdeacon in captivity—and, by the way, that may explain his way of addressing you—wanted us to have the archdeacon *motif* in our minds, so to speak—here's a captive archdeacon inviting us to consider whether archdeacons can be saved, and telling us the answer is Yes! In other words, he's saying to us Can't you rescue this particular Archdeacon?"

"I agree with your explanation," said Birtley, "and it may be worth while to remark that the reference to Mr. and Mrs. Wilson must have been inserted to make sure that we did not miss the point, as I understand that it was they who raised the question when you discussed it."

"No doubt of that," said Wilson.

"That's all very well so far," said Pycroft, "but it wants a lot more thinking out. All that we can say up to date is that he believes a rescue is possible, and we've got to try to find out how it can be done."

"In view of our complete ignorance whether the brigands took them north or south I can't say that the prospect is very encouraging," remarked Birtley.

"I do wish he could have given us some sort of hint," lamented the archdeacon.

"Wouldn't have been any too easy", remarked Wilson, "with the chief brigand probably standing over him when he wrote. The chap who organized this business is bound to be a brainy fellow, and he wouldn't let anything pass."

"Well, Craggs is no fool either," said Pycroft. "Let's try and see if he's managed to slip in any sort of hint."

The Letter

They read the letter through again with meticulous care.

"It is obvious they're pretty high up somewhere", said Wilson, "or he wouldn't have put in that bit about their being lame when they got there."

"In view of the mountains which enclose the valley on either side", said Mr. Birtley, coldly, "that cannot be called a very valuable indication: it is much as if a man kidnapped in the Sahara were to say that he was writing from a somewhat sandy area."

"I don't understand why he put in the bit about being 'nearly blind'," said Pycroft. "It's quite true it was a sunny day when they were captured, but the sun wasn't as bad as all that."

"I suppose it might have got worse as they went up the mountain," suggested Wilson.

"It might, though you'd hardly expect it; it all depends which way they went; and we've no line on that at all."

"The inefficiency of the Greek police is almost incredible," remarked Mr. Birtley. "After first declaring that there were no brigands at all in the district, they have veered round, under pressure, to maintaining that all the mountains to north, south and east are so thickly infested with them that it is quite impossible to suggest which is the best direction for a search."

"I don't believe they've made anything worth calling a search in any direction at all," said Wilson. "I never saw a more rascally looking lot, and their chief boss seems frankly gaga!"

The archdeacon had taken no part in the discussion for some little time. "Do you know," he said at length, "I really do think I have got just the faintest shadow of an idea: it is so very vague that I hardly like to mention it."

"Let's have it for what it may be worth," said Pycroft. "Every little helps."

"Well," began Castleton, with much diffidence. "You know the combination of the words 'lame' and 'blind' seemed to suggest something to me. You will remember how 'the lame and the blind' came to Our Lord in the Temple, and I wondered…"

"By Jove, Castleton, I believe you've hit it," cried Pycroft. "You mean they've been taken to some famous old temple, and he thinks we'll know where it is."

"That did just occur to me as a possibility," said the archdeacon, modestly.

"As far as I know," said Mr. Birtley, "the only famous temple in these parts is Bassae: it's certainly famous enough, but I think it's a long way off."

"I'll get a map," said Wilson, and returned with an ancient classical atlas which, by the advice of Professor Tomkins, he had purchased in Athens. They pored over it together.

"Here it is—down just above Messenia—it's a deuce of a way off though—thirty miles or so as the crow flies, and goodness knows how many more by road, even if there were any roads. I can't see any sort of track leading to it from the north."

"I seem to remember that a friend of mine who went there came up from the east," said Mr. Birtley: "It looks rather more approachable from that side."

"I hardly see how they could have got them there in the time," said Pycroft, "let alone getting their messenger back here; and there's another thing against it. As you say, tourists do go there, and they'd hardly want to run the risk of running into them. Aren't there any other temples about?"

"None that I've ever heard of—but let's have a look at the map."

But the map failed to disclose any other sacred sites in the neighbourhood.

"We might make inquiries of the local people—meanwhile I'm afraid Bassae's a wash-out. Sorry, Castleton—it was quite worth trying."

Discouragement descended on the party once more.

The Letter

"I'm afraid it's no good," said Wilson. "But after all we've only got to pay the money and they'll be sent back: Craggs practically says so."

"Yes, assuming that the brigands can be trusted."

"He doesn't suggest they can't."

"He couldn't, very well, in a letter their chief was going to read. No," went on Pycroft, "I'm all for paying up—of course we'll do that anyhow and hope for the best. But Craggs says he wants to be *rescued:* he wouldn't have taken all this trouble if he simply wanted the money paid. I'm not going to give up without another try to find out what he *did* mean."

"I'm all for that," said Wilson, "once it's decided to pay the money."

"Of course it is: no one ever disputed that, but, as I see it, we've got an off-chance of bagging the brigands as well, if only we can find out where they are. Now, Castleton, you've had one very good idea: can't you produce another?"

The archdeacon, thus encouraged, was emboldened to try again. "There *is* another place in the Bible", he said, with more diffidence than ever, "where the lame and the blind are mentioned together. It comes in the Second Book of Samuel, as no doubt you will remember: I ought perhaps to add that the precise meaning of the passage is disputed—but it says that, when David was attacking the city of the Jebusites, they did say that only the lame and the blind could get up there. I fancy what they really said was that it was such a strong place that the lame and the blind would be enough to hold it. I confess that I cannot see how it helps us, but, as you ask me, I thought it might be just worth mentioning."

"Thanks very much," said Pycroft, "quite worth mentioning, though I can't see that it leads to much at the moment: what was the name of the place?"

The Letter

"I fancy its old name was Jebus, and that the Jebusites took their name from it."

"Jebus? Jebus? No, I can't see how that comes into the picture—not a very likely name for a place in these parts."

Mr. Birtley had been idly looking at the letter again. "Is it not conceivable", he asked, "that we have here the explanation of that curious signature: J. B. S. Craggs? J. B. S.—Jebus? May not that be the hint we were looking for?"

"Bravo, Birtley. I rather think you've done it this time! Let's have another go at the map."

But an intensive survey of the ancient atlas, and of the more modern maps in *Baedeker,* revealed no name which could by any stretch of the imagination be connected with Jebus.

Their hopes having been raised so high by Birtley's discovery, the ensuing depression was equally great, and they sat in gloomy silence for a few minutes, wondering where next to turn. By this time they were all convinced that a message lay in the letter, and they racked their brains for a possible solution.

The silence was at last broken by the gentle voice of the archdeacon. "Of course", he said, "you all know, when David took the city, he gave it the name of Zion, which was afterwards to become so famous."

"That doesn't sound very like Greek to me," said Wilson, whose discouragement was the most apparent.

"Hold on a moment," said Pycroft: "I'm sure I came across something very like it when we were hunting through the map just now.

"Yes, here you are! Mt. Lasion, a spur of Mt. Pholoe, not more than fifteen miles from this valley, and just north of the next one. On the map it looks just the sort of place they might make for. Castleton, what a thing it is to be a Biblical scholar! I really believe you've saved the situation."

The Letter

Pycroft's enthusiasm was contagious; Wilson warmly supported him, and, though both Birtley and Castleton were more dubious, both were impressed by the fact that a level-headed Yorkshireman had committed himself to a decision so obviously chancy. Besides, action of any sort was clearly preferable to the enforced inactivity of the last twenty-four hours, and they were all convinced that Craggs's letter showed both that he expected some attempt at rescue, and that he had good hopes that it might succeed.

Though it was well past midnight, it was decided to get in touch with the captain at once, and with his help to organize such forces as were available for an advance on Mt. Lasion next day.

The archdeacon suddenly remembered that he had never read the instructions, which had indeed been completely forgotten in the excitement of their attempt to solve the problem of the letter.

"Ought we to read them now, do you think?" he asked.

"I'm too tired," said Pycroft, "besides, they're sure to be only formal: let's wait till we've seen the captain."

"I may remark", said Mr. Birtley, before they finally left the smoking room, having sent a sleepy steward to awaken the captain on urgent business, "I may remark that the events of this evening have permanently raised my opinion of archdeacons as a class. I know not whether the ingenuity displayed by the Archdeacon of Thorp in composing his letter, or the patience and erudition shown by the Archdeacon of Garminster in contributing so greatly to its solution is worthy of the higher praise. Gentlemen, I give you the toast of the Archidiaconate of the Church of England!"

CHAPTER XV

Preparations

"A wise stout captain and persuaded."
—Shakespeare

The captain was far from pleased at being disturbed so late, and let the fact be clearly seen. The blunt straightforwardness of the seafaring man has been often and deservedly held up to admiration, and it may be said at once that no fault could be found with either the bluntness or the straightforwardness of his remarks to his visitors. He inquired of a just Providence whether it was not sufficient punishment for his sins to be stuck off a mouldy little harbour, at the mercy of a pack of unmentionable Greeks, without being kicked up in the dead of night by—— Here he caught the mild but reproving eye of the archdeacon, and moderated his tone.

He said, moreover, that he ought certainly to have been told at once, and was only gradually appeased by Pycroft's assurance that they had only (as they believed) solved the riddle a quarter of an hour before. He was at first extremely sceptical as to their interpretation, and it took some time to persuade him that their deductions were sound, but he had considerable respect for Pycroft's judgment, being (perhaps fortunately) a good Yorkshireman himself. Moreover, as we have seen, he was extremely anxious to get away from the inadequate anchorage, and their plan offered at least a possibility of getting the matter settled.

Preparations

So much being agreed, they now proceeded to read the typewritten paper of instructions: it ran as follows:

1. The sum of £450 (four hundred & fifty pounds) to be provided in English, Greek or French money—the exchange to be taken at the day's current value. Any shortage in the amount will cause delay and inconvenience.
2. The bearer of the money to walk alone along the road leading north from the harbour station, starting at 10 o'clock. He will, in due course, be met by a man who will present as his credentials a typewritten copy of these instructions. The exchange of the copies will be regarded as proof that the transaction has been completed.
3. Any attempt to watch the interview, or to follow the messenger, or in any way to observe his movements, will result in serious inconvenience (and further expense) to the persons detained.
4. As soon as the messenger returns with the money, immediate steps will be taken to return them to their friends.

"The only question is", said Pycroft, "can the purser produce the money?"

"I'm sure he can," said the captain, "if the passengers will co-operate, as no doubt they will. The Company will be ready to help, assuming of course that you will give them an indemnity. If we can't raise the money on the ship, we can raise it on shore. But which of you gentlemen is going to take charge of it?"

"Of course I shall be very ready, if you wish it," said Castleton, "but I really feel that Mr. Pycroft would be much better, if he would be kind enough to undertake it. It may be necessary to talk to the messenger, and though I *might* learn how to say £450 in Greek, I doubt if I could say it in a way he would understand."

So it was finally agreed, and they turned to the steps to be taken to prepare for the attack on Mt. Lasion.

Preparations

"There's no doubt our strongest card is the Greek troops," said Pycroft. "I believe they can be trusted: if we use the police, I think one or two of us ought to be there to make sure there's no hanky panky."

"There's another point," began Birtley.

"Now, gentlemen, gentlemen!" said the captain, yawning. "It's close on 2 o'clock, and we've all got a busy day before us. There's nothing to be done before morning, and the sooner we're all of us in bed the better. I'll co-operate in every way I can, for it's the best chance I see, but I tell you frankly my co-operation won't be worth much if I can't keep my eyes open. So good night to you all!"

He ushered them politely but firmly out of his cabin—but Birtley was not to be done out of his point.

"Why in the world did none of us notice that the amount ought to be £550 and not £450?" he asked. "£100 each and £50 for Miss Hillcroft."

"Yes, and now I remember Craggs said £450 too," said Castleton, "but no one noticed it then; we were so busy about the rest of his letter: can it be a mistake?"

"Not likely," said Pycroft, "they wouldn't both get the figure wrong: all the same, perhaps I'd better take another £100 with me, to be on the safe side."

Birtley urged that, as they had the figure twice down in black and white, this was unnecessary, but Wilson was determined that no risk of delay should be run, and offered himself to be responsible for the extra amount.

"I cannot think what it means," said the archdeacon. "We know it cannot be Craggs who is missing, or Mrs. Wilson, or Miss Hillcroft; that leaves Lady Mary, Mrs. Burslem and Michalis."

"Surely he'd have said if any of them had had an accident. I'm too sleepy to think at all," said Pycroft: "as the captain said, we've got a busy day before us."

Preparations

The next day was indeed full of occupation. The purser had to collect the money, which proved unexpectedly easy: Pycroft had to be conveyed to the harbour to keep his appointment: he subsequently reported that £450 was apparently all that was demanded.

During his absence preparations were pushed rapidly forward, and indeed he was only just in time to join one of the assaulting parties. These were divided into three. The Greek police, stiffened by the presence of Wilson, Birtley and two other stalwart passengers, were to approach by the western path to the mountain top, while the Greek soldiers, with whom were Pycroft, the major and the archdeacon, approached it on the right. The ship's company provided a third force to encompass the mountains in the rear with Mr. Ryland to assist in securing synchronization. Yet a further body of skirmishers, composed of the younger Hellenic travellers, had a roving commission to cover any unknown tracks which might be discovered. Their elders were allowed, if they wished, to attach themselves to any of the regular forces, while Miss Bustard, with great efficiency, organized the more lissom of the ladies into a commissariat department, carrying supplies of extra food and drink, and prepared to render first aid to any wounded heroes.

The archdeacon was deservedly accommodated with a mule, and another was assigned to Professor Tomkins in his capacity of War correspondent. This was, of course, before the day when England had become accustomed to Combined Military Operations, and it may safely be said that no force so varied in its composition and so ardent in its enthusiasm had ever been launched from the deck of the S.S. *Lucretia*.

CHAPTER XVI

Michalis

"He was a man of a strange temperament."
Byron—*Don Juan*

The day passed drearily for the captives, on whom even the beauty of the survey was beginning to pall, as the food had long since done: the polite messages from Mr. Michalis by which it was accompanied did nothing to make it more palatable. Mrs. Burslem, though promoted from Ezra Pound to T. S. Eliot, had developed no taste for modern poetry, and made little of a copy of *Wuthering Heights* which Craggs had discovered in Michalis's motley library. Mrs. Wilson was teaching Spiro English: Lady Mary passed her time in sulky silence, declaring that she was too ill either to speak or to read, but the fact that the detective story which Phyllis was reading—*Murder on the Backstairs*—was found under her pillow after a prolonged siesta threw some doubt on the latter part of her statement.

After tea—a meal which, in fact, consisted of quite palatable coffee—Craggs went to pay another visit to Michalis, whose conversation he found entertaining: as he left the ladies' cave he heard Mrs. Wilson's voice saying patiently, "No, Spiro, not 'standed'—'stood'," and Spiro's triumphant reply, "I stooded".

"I do hope the ladies haven't been too uncomfortable," was Michalis's first inquiry.

He had been amused to hear of Mrs. Burslem's struggles with modern verse and confessed that privately he shared her opinion: Craggs, who was something of a modernist, had hotly protested, and they had had an animated discussion which he was now hoping to renew; but Michalis went off on another subject.

"I forgot to ask if you had much bother about that money question?" he said. "It was really very inconsiderate of me to give you the dirty work to do!"

Craggs told him that Lady Mary had given some trouble, and explained what had happened.

"Yes, she's a mean old thing," remarked Michalis: "She's not rich, but she's not as poor as all that: I used to know a nephew of hers once, and I've heard him talk of her. I expect he'll have to pay up for her in the end, but I'm glad to think he's a duke now and can easily afford it—so that doesn't worry me. But I don't like the idea of you and Mrs. Wilson having to pay for Miss Hillcroft: I really think we'd better let her off altogether. You'd better not tell her—Miss Hillcroft, I mean, but I shouldn't like you to be out of pocket."

It is a little difficult to know just how grateful one ought to be to a brigand who proposes first to rob and then to tip you, and Craggs was somewhat at a loss: he was just beginning to murmur his thanks at the unexpected suggestion when Michalis went on:

"As a matter of fact, I've done much better out of this than I expected: I've had a chance of looking through Mrs. Burslem's stuff, and it's really very good indeed. Besides those pearls she was always wearing—and they're first-rate of course—there were two or three really good rings, so I can easily afford it!"

"You'll be glad to hear she's well insured," said Craggs. "She even seemed to think she'll make a little on the transaction."

"What did I tell you?" said Michalis. "She's the sort of Woman it's a real pleasure to rob, when one once forgets the conventions: but, by the way, I'd better send her back those things she bought at Olympia—she can't very well have insured them. You can tell her they're all quite genuine."

"I rather think she'd like a written guarantee," said Craggs, laughing.

"Oh, anything to oblige!" and he scribbled on a piece of paper in a flourishing hand, "*Garantito*, Michalis" and handed it to the archdeacon with the parcel—"The Italian adds just a tinge of romance, I think."

"Lady Mary's another robber's joy, though for rather different reasons," he resumed.

"Mrs. Wilson's quite well off, I know—and you will tell me quite frankly, won't you, if it's in the least inconvenient to you?"

Craggs burst out laughing.

"You really are the most unusual type of brigand!" he said. "No, I shall get over it all right: I only hope your 'good causes' are good enough! But I wish you'd tell me how you came to take to this kind of job?"

Michalis smiled a little, and hesitated for a moment before replying. "Well, it's a queer thing to say, but I really think it all came from the French I learnt, or rather didn't learn, at school."

"What in the world do you mean?"

"Well, for one thing, we read *Le Roi des Montagnes*—perhaps you'd have guessed I'd read that—and for another, the chap who taught us French was full of brigand stories—we used to say he must have been a pirate himself, and I used to lap them up. I wish I'd paid as much attention to his French lessons as I did to his yarns—then I shouldn't have had so much trouble with my French idioms on the boat. A queer chap he was," he went on. "He used to keep a telescope, and have a look round from the roof of his house, just as if he'd been at sea—I remember he spotted a boy smoking once about five miles off—he behaved very well about that."

Craggs had been listening open-mouthed.

"You don't mean to say you were at Eton?" he gasped.

"Ah, you remembered that little episode? I thought you would.

Of course I was wondering how soon you'd catch on!"

"Don't tell me you were there with me?"

Michalis's manner completely changed; dropping the semi-itonic manner he had employed, he became completely natural.

"Most certainly I was," he said, laughing. "I knew you quite well by sight, but you wouldn't remember me. You were a great swell—Sixth Form, Pop. the XI and so on, when I was a Lower Boy. I very well remember that 50 you made against Winchester. I was always very keen on cricket myself, though I was never any good. That's one of the disadvantages of this job—one never gets the chance of seeing any decent cricket," he ended, with a sigh.

"Where did you board?" asked Craggs.

"No, I'm not going to tell you that. It might make things a bit awkward for both of us: not that I'd mind your knowing my name, but on the whole it's better not: my people wouldn't like it for one thing—they think I've just got a passion for travelling. They believe I'm in Japan at the moment: I get letters sent there regularly from Japan saying how I'm getting on: it was a fearful job mugging up Japanese geography enough to make it sound plausible. So I think we'll leave it at that.

"But do tell me some Eton shop: I couldn't get down the last time I was in England. What sort of a side have we got this year?"

And probably for the first time in its age-long history Mt. Lasion listened to an animated discussion of the prospects of a match at Lords. Craggs was fully alive to the absurdity of the position, and, in the intervals of discussing Eton XI's of the past, was endeavouring to set in order his impressions of his host. He was a very good actor, that was clear, but what was the character of the man himself? Were Mrs. Burslem's pearls really going to support good causes? He more than half believed it, though Blades certainly took some explaining away. At any rate there was no doubt either that Michalis thoroughly enjoyed his present life, or that he had considerable knowledge of the game of cricket. The time passed happily away: they were still hard at it when a brigand appeared with a message delivered in Greek: Michalis answered in the same language.

"This is Dmitri," he said, turning to the archdeacon. "Dmitri, this is Mr. Craggs."

"Pleased to meetcha, Mr. Craggs," said the Americanized Dmitri, with a friendly grin. "All O.K. with you?"

"Send him in at once, Dmitri," said Michalis, and when he had gone, he went on:

"That's very satisfactory. The messenger's got back, so I hope all is well."

The messenger, another brigand almost indistinguishable from Dmitri, now appeared, bearing a large envelope which he delivered to his leader. Michalis opened it, examined the contents, and asked a few questions of the bearer, who was then dismissed.

"That seems all right," he said. "Of course the money will need careful checking, but they seem to have calculated the exchange at a very reasonable rate. I asked the man to describe the person who brought it, and it seems to have been your friend Pycroft—I always liked his looks."

"Then we can get off at once?" asked Craggs.

"As early as you like to-morrow: I'll try to get some more mules."

At this moment he was interrupted by the arrival of yet a third brigand who delivered a message with much gesticulation. Michalis gave him some orders and dismissed him: then he turned to Craggs, resuming as he did so the semi-ironic manner which he had temporarily laid aside.

"That really is something of a nuisance. It seems that the Greek police are at the foot of the mountain. It's nothing serious of course, but they feel bound to make a demonstration in force if any considerable fuss is made, naturally giving us notice of the way by which they are coming: their commandant is a very trustworthy fellow. But I'm afraid that means that I must go and change, and that we must break off our talk. It needn't bother you at all. I'm afraid they'll have a hot climb, but the poor fellows do deserve some encouragement, and they'll get a lot of credit out of it, besides what they get from us. They won't be here for a couple of hours at the least. I can't tell you how I've enjoyed our talk: I wish I could have kept you a day or two longer, but I'm afraid that mightn't have suited you!

"Oh, by the way, I've just remembered one thing I must ask you to do. Would you mind collecting any paper—old letters and such things—all paper, in fact, in the possession of yourself and the others? That is a rule we always have to make. You will realize that it is very undesirable that any record should exist of this little episode, however fragmentary. I am sure you will do it more tactfully than any of my own people, who, I am afraid, might be a little heavy-handed. I need not say that you can assure the ladies that I should not dream of reading any of their private correspondence: it is merely a simple matter of precaution."

Craggs departed on his errand, revolving many things in his mind. On his arrival he first performed the pleasanter part of his errand. Mrs. Burslem, as he expected, was delighted to recover her purchases, and enchanted with the guarantee.

"I must say I call that very friendly of him," she said. "I always knew there was some good in him, whatever people might say"—with a bitter glance at Lady Mary. "There's not a pair of Burslem's braces in Manchester to-day that doesn't carry its own detachable guarantee—and not one of them ever claimed either," she added, in a burst of honesty, "for everyone loses them at once: my poor husband made a great point of it," though it remained uncertain whether it was the guarantee or its detachability to which the late Mr. Burslem had attached special importance.

In the matter of the written matter, as he expected, he met with the strongest opposition from Lady Mary, who protested that she had in her bag a very private letter from the Duchess which she could not dream of submitting to alien eyes. The difficulty was solved by Craggs devoting one of his few remaining matches, and the precious document was ceremonially consumed. The others raised no objection, and he returned with the letters in a largish packet. As he neared Michalis's cave he saw Blades come rushing up from the other side and calling loudly for his chief. Craggs decided to take cover behind a tree and to see what was happening. In a moment, Michalis appeared in the mouth of the cave: he was obviously in the process of changing his clothes—he had discarded his shooting jacket and his nether limbs were clothed in the native kilt.

"What's the matter?" he asked.

"It's the soldiers," cried Blades. "They're coming up the other side."

"Nonsense! What would they be doing here?"

"They're coming all right! Come and look for yourself."

Michalis, half dressed as he was, hurried out of the cave, and the pair of them disappeared round the shelter of the mountain.

"Stung with the splendour of a sudden thought," Craggs hurried into the cave and passed behind the curtain. A minute was enough for him to do what he wanted: he hurried out again, and disappeared among the trees. Some desultory shots were beginning to be heard from below.

There we will leave him, and will turn to look at the incidents of this eventful day from another point of view.

CHAPTER XVII

The Great Assault

"All this is very fine, and may be true."
                                                                                                                   BYRON—*DON JUAN*

For this purpose we can hardly do better than quote from the account which Professor Tomkins compiled, and subsequently delivered as a lecture on board the *Lucretia*: of the many lectures which he had delivered, none had received a warmer welcome from a more crowded audience.

It is unfortunately impossible to guarantee the verbal accuracy of the report: true, it was compiled from shorthand notes taken on the spot by a young lady Hellenic Traveller; but on the other hand, she was a pupil of Miss Bustard, who—alas, that such rancour should live in academic minds!—had been known privately to describe the Professor as a "pompous and pretentious wind-bag", and her pupil may have imbibed some of her preceptor's prejudice.

We need not linger over the earlier passages, in which he gave a full account of the events leading up to the capture, passing regretfully over the treachery of Michalis—"a wolf, we may say, clad in the innocent sheepskin of a Hellenic Traveller": he paid a glowing tribute to the skill of Archdeacon Craggs ("as we are now at liberty to call him") in composing his letter, and of Archdeacon Castleton in making its dark places plain. His learned digression on the growth and functions of the Archdeaconate had been heard in decorous silence, but there were slight signs of restiveness before he turned to more modern days.

"We have seen, ladies and gentlemen, these admirable functionaries performing with competence their allotted task: to-day we pay homage to their versatility as men of affairs—men skilled to plan a daring enterprise and to carry it to a triumphant conclusion."

His account of the heroic endurance of the captives—"ladies, diverse perhaps in age and station, but united in resolve—true specimens of British womanhood"—was extremely moving, for there had been agreement to conceal the extreme unwillingness which one of them had displayed to take her share of discomfort, but it was generally agreed that he touched his highest point as an orator when dealing with the military aspects of the affair.

He began by drawing an unfavourable comparison between the Trojan war and that recently concluded, for while the former had taken its origin from the abduction of Helen—"a woman beautiful indeed, but, in a very real sense of the word, a single woman"—the brigands had carried into captivity no less than four: "the one struggle lasted no less than ten years: the other was victoriously ended in a single day."

"Who that saw it can forget the majesty with which the gallant soldiers of the King of the Hellenes marched forth on their heroic mission? It was a small body, it is true, no more than fifty, which Captain Demetriadi led forth into the mountains, but when have mere numbers been the criterion of military distinction? There came, I cannot but believe, to every mind the recollection of the glories of Marathon, where, by the sacrifice of 192 brave men, the people of Athens routed the myriads of the Persians and changed the destiny of Europe.

"Nor was there lacking to the expedition a peculiar honour of its own. We saw, marching by the side of our allies, a

The Great Assault

major in the British Army, Major Thisleton, crowning a life of service to king and country by this final act of sacrifice. He had waived his superiority of rank, and was content to serve as a volunteer under a simple captain, recalling truly those great acts of self-abnegation which, in other centuries and in other lands, have added lustre to the name of the British soldier.

"With him there marched Archdeacon Castleton, a man venerable in every sense of the word, acting for the nonce as Chaplain to the Forces, bearing indeed no weapons of war, but by his presence an inspiration to the troops. Mules, in the past, have carried popes and prelates, but I venture to assert that there lives no prouder mule to-day than that which had the honour to bear our friend the Archdeacon of Garminster. On the left wing marched a detachment of the gallant Greek police, representing that co-operation of the civil and military powers on which the security of a country so eminently depends.

"Nor was the Navy without its representatives: the *Lucretia* herself, though not a vessel of war, supplied a contingent to watch the northern slopes, a body which could be trusted to maintain the honour of the Senior Service: and what shall I say of the passengers themselves? There was not one of them who, if age and infirmity permitted, was not ready and anxious to play his part: the value of a skirmishing force, light armed indeed, but mobile in the extreme, can never be underrated in such an enterprise as this. The haul of prisoners taken is a sufficient proof of their efficiency: and finally let me pay my homage to our Amazons, who under the able organization of Miss Bustard, rendered invaluable service in supplying those creature comforts without which so arduous an expedition could never have been brought to a successful issue."

The Great Assault

At this point, Professor Tomkins described at length the difficulties of the ascent, the heat of the day, the exhaustion of the assailing force, and the ministrations of Miss Bustard's band: we must hasten to his account of the actual fighting.

"The right wing, the soldiers, were, as was fitting, the first to come into action. Climbing the precipitous rock, they sighted, and were themselves sighted by, the brigands who held the almost inaccessible crests. A dropping fire was interchanged, in the course of which a serious loss was inflicted on the enemy, for the superior marksmanship of the military had its just reward. In the earliest stages of the engagement, a bullet pierced the heart of Mr. Blades, and his fall disorganized the enemy's resistance in this quarter.

"There is an old saying, *De mortuis nil nisi bonum*, and I cannot bring myself to exult over his death, or to describe the acts by which, as I must feel, he had deserved it: it is enough for me to say that for such a man to pose as a member of the Hellenic Travellers' Club was an indecency which has thus met a not unfitting retribution. With his fall, the task of the troops became comparatively simple.

"Foreseeing this, your correspondent—if I may arrogate to myself so honourable a title—made his way round, with considerable difficulty owing to the unaccountable conduct of his mule, to the other, or western, side of the mountain.

"Here a still sterner struggle was in progress: the brigands resisted fiercely, and there were moments when the brave police seemed to be incapable of forcing their way upwards. At this moment—the very crisis of the battle—one of their officers, whom it has unfortunately proved impossible to identify, saved the situation by an act of rare gallantry. Rallying his men, and himself the foremost in the assault, he cleared the brigands from the heights, and stood for a moment triumphant on the hill.

The object attained, he merged himself once more among his men, and left to them the honour of the final triumph.

"You will wish, I am sure, to join with me in paying homage to this act of selfless gallantry, which has added fresh lustre to the annals of the Greek police. I can assure you that I personally made every effort to discover his name, but my imperfect knowledge of the Greek language, combined with the regrettable eccentricities of my mule, made the task impossible in view of his determination to remain unknown. I can only say that I count it a privilege to have witnessed so noble a deed, and that I only wish I were able to pay to him in person that mark of honour which he so gloriously earned."

After this, the professor proceeded to describe in detail the rescue of the captives, the counting of the (three) prisoners taken and the triumphant return to the ship.

Craggs and Castleton had sat at the back of the room during the lecture, the better to conceal their blushes. When it was over, they strolled together on the deck.

"The professor enjoyed himself, I think!" said the Archdeacon of Garminster.

"Yes, he fairly let himself go," responded Craggs.

"I wonder who that Greek policeman was," said Castleton. "I cannot say that any of those whom I saw looked particularly heroic."

"Oh, didn't you guess? That was Michalis, of course."

"Michalis?" cried his companion, in amazement.

"Oh, yes, I knew that all along. I didn't say anything about it, for fear of spoiling the professor's fun. You see, he was dressing up as a policeman when I saw him last, much the best disguise he could have taken. He'll have slipped away easily when the fighting was over, and I can't say I'm sorry. I confess I had a queer sort of liking for the chap in spite of everything."

"But what about the rest of the brigands?" asked Castleton.

The Great Assault

"Oh, I expect they merged imperceptibly into the police: they were in very close touch with them all along: I've no doubt Dmitri's back in his bank all right: I believe they think very well of him there."

"But the prisoners?" objected the Archdeacon of Garminster.

"Ah, they weren't brigands at all—I knew that as soon as I saw them—but quite genuine goatherds. I fancy Michalis employs them as 'supers' at a small retaining fee, and they're always ready to be captured if necessary."

"But surely there will be an inquiry?" said Castleton.

"Who's to make it? The Greeks won't—the less fuss there is, the less damage there'll be to the tourist business: we certainly shan't—do you see the captain hanging on for an interminable argument in a Greek law court? Oh, no, Michalis had everything very well worked out. He's an extremely capable chap, and I'm not at all sure that he isn't an honest man, though I daresay you find that pretty hard to believe."

"Well, you knew him very much better than I did," answered Castleton, "but I do not quite like to think that he has scored all along the line, as one might say."

"Not quite all along the line," said Craggs. "He's got a little surprise coming to him—but I won't tell even you about that now. I want a shot in my locker for that insufferable old Lady Mary, and I mean to loose it off to-morrow!"

CHAPTER XVIII

Lady Mary's Dilemma

"A sudden conflict rises from the swell."
—Wordsworth

Lady Mary, who had not attended the lecture—she had indeed remained in her cabin ever since her return—employed her time in writing a long letter to the captain. As Phyllis Hillcroft was given the task of transcribing it, she had no difficulty in communicating its contents to Craggs: he was therefore not surprised to be summoned by the captain to discuss the matter. To him he explained the whole situation, for, as has been said, they were on excellent terms, and it was arranged that Lady Mary should be invited (if her health permitted) to attend a conference in the captain's quarters on the following day.

This, somewhat to their surprise, she consented to do, and invitations were also issued to her fellow captives, and to the Archdeacon of Garminster. They, with the exception of Phyllis, were in their places in good time and some five minutes afterwards her ladyship appeared, attended by her escort.

The captain was in high good humour; for one thing, he had got away earlier than he expected, for another, the weather was all that he could wish, and lastly he had had satisfactory news as to accommodation in the French harbour for which they were bound. He anticipated an amusing interview.

He arose, as they all did, at Lady Mary's arrival, and greeted her with respectful warmth.

"I am sure it is very good of you to come, Lady Mary," he said. "I know what you have been through, and am very grateful to you for having made the effort."

Lady Mary replied that only a sense of public duty could have enabled her to rise superior to her sufferings.

"Quite so! Quite so! Now let me find you a comfortable seat. As you see, I have invited your fellow captives to be here, as you will, no doubt, wish them to hear what you have to say? And Archdeacon Castleton, too, to represent Mr. Craggs, as I understand from your letter that you have some serious accusations to bring against him."

Lady Mary graciously signified her assent to these arrangements. She proceeded to say that she had, in fact, very serious complaints to make against Mr. Craggs, whose behaviour she considered quite inexcusable. "One would have thought", she said, "that any man of breedin', findin' himself in a responsible position, would at least have done his best for the rest of us. To find oneself at the mercy of a man with no consideration for others, and himself a man of no position——"

"Forgive me, Lady Mary," said the captain, "but you understand, don't you, that Mr. Craggs is, in fact, the Archdeacon of Thorp?"

"I am sure", said Castleton, gently, "that Lady Mary would be the last to suggest that the possession or otherwise of any title, whether personal or official, makes any difference to one's responsibilities."

Lady Mary, momentarily a little deflated, changed her ground with some dexterity.

"That is precisely what I was sayin'," she said, boldly disregarding the facts, "that a man holdin' a responsible position should act so inconsiderately makes the matter ten times worse."

"You remember, Lady Mary", said the captain, "that, had it not been for the Archdeacon of Thorp, you and all the rest of the party would still be in the hands of the brigands?"

"That may, or may not, be so," returned Lady Mary, "I know nothin' about it" (which indeed was true). "What I do know is that, instead of lookin' after our interests, he was hobnobbin' with that scoundrel Michalis, and probably bargainin' with him for a share of the ransom."

"Forgive me one moment," put in Castleton. "Captain, may I ask you to make a note of those words? They clearly constitute slander of the most serious kind. I have, of course, no idea whether my friend will wish to bring an action, but it is obvious that, if he does, Lady Mary would be liable for very heavy damages. I shall, therefore, be grateful if a note can be made."

"Certainly," said the captain, who proceeded to write busily.

The pause, and the mention of possible heavy damages, gave Lady Mary time and matter for reflection: when she next spoke, it was in a somewhat less truculent tone.

"I don't wish to be bringin' any charges," she said. "I'm only sayin' what it looked like to me. In any case there's no doubt that it was thanks to him that we were let in for payin' a preposterous sum to that friend of Mrs. Burslem's."

She shot a venomous glance in her direction as she spoke, and Mrs. Burslem began a vehement retort.

"Pardon me, Mrs. Burslem," said Castleton, "perhaps you will allow me first to invite Lady Mary to elucidate her remark? Do I understand you to suggest that Mrs. Burslem also was in league with Mr. Michalis? That would also, I fancy, be clearly actionable."

"I don't say she was in league with him," said her ladyship, sulkily. "I only say that, but for her makin' such a friend of him, none of these things would have happened."

"I think", said the captain, "that we are rather wandering from the point: what precisely is the accusation you wish to bring against Archdeacon Craggs?"

"I say that he could at any rate have made better terms for us. Some people" (with another venomous glance at Mrs.

Burslem) "may not mind throwin' their money away: I say we ought to have been asked."

"But I understood that you *were* consulted," said the captain: "perhaps on that point we might hear what the other ladies have to say."

They all agreed that Lady Mary, as well as themselves, had had the whole situation put before them, and had agreed to the terms proposed: it was only with the greatest difficulty that two of them were prevented from enlarging on Lady Mary's unwillingness to co-operate and on the meanness of her attitude towards Miss Hillcroft.

"I couldn't help agreein'," said Lady Mary more sulkily than ever, "but that doesn't alter the fact that better terms should have been got. My nephew the Duke knows the Bishop of Thorp well, and I shall certainly see that the matter is brought to his notice."

"That will not be necessary," said Craggs, speaking for the first time. "Your nephew and I were in the same house at Eton, and I shall be only too glad to talk the whole matter over with him. I hope he is well? I have hardly seen him since he went to Cambridge, but we saw a lot of one another in old days."

This entirely unexpected revelation took Lady Mary between wind and water. She was for a moment at a loss for a reply, and Craggs proceeded to press his advantage.

"Is there any other accusation, Captain?" he asked—"it would be convenient to have the whole business cleared up at once."

"Yes," said the captain. "I think there is something about some letters which Lady Mary says were forcibly taken from her."

Her ladyship had had time to recover.

"Yes," she cried, "a most ungentlemanly act! That is a point which I think will need some explainin'!"

"You will remember, Lady Mary", said Craggs, "that I burnt in your presence the only letter which you regarded as private."

"But why take them at all? You were actin' under the orders of that ruffian, even if you weren't a friend of his."

"There", said the archdeacon, "I have a little surprise for you which I hope you will regard as pleasant. I was able to take the opportunity of substituting that parcel of letters for the notes which Michalis had received in payment of the ransom. Here they are. Would you prefer to receive your £100 in Greek or French currency? I might even be able to manage it in English money."

He produced the envelope as he spoke.

The love of money, if not the root of all Lady Mary's evil, was at least a substantial part of her moral make-up. The thought of unexpectedly recovering £100, which she had regarded as irretrievably lost, finally broke down her resistance.

"English money, please," she muttered, and, as the notes were placed in her hands, she was distinctly heard to murmur "Thank you!"

"Well, that is all very satisfactorily settled," said the captain, rising. "I feel that the rest of you ladies would wish to join in the vote of thanks which Lady Mary has been good enough to propose? Thank you, I thought as much. Archdeacon, it gives me great pleasure to convey it to you, and to add my own gratitude for all your services to us all, and to the *Lucretia*. Now, Lady Mary, I am sure you ought to be going to rest: let me thank you again for your courtesy in coming here."

He bowed her ceremoniously out of the cabin. When the door was closed, he turned to the Archdeacon of Thorp.

"Went like clockwork, didn't it? Shocking old party, what?"

"You did your part nobly," said Craggs. "I thought that would be the way to make her see reason."

"I do call that clever of you, Mr. Craggs—Archdeacon Craggs, I should say," said Mrs. Burslem. "I only wish you could have known my poor dear husband! You're a man after his own heart! There was no trick in business he didn't know."

Craggs bowed his acknowledgment of this rather ambiguous testimonial, and turned to receive the thanks of Mrs. Wilson, whose shares had risen distinctly in his estimation since her behaviour on the mountain.

"I wish Phyllis could have stayed to thank you too," she said. "However, she had the pleasure of seeing that old cat put in her place for once!"

It was not till later in the evening, when it could fairly be hoped that Lady Mary was safely tucked up for the night, that Phyllis got the opportunity of expressing her gratitude.

"I do think it was kind of you and Mrs. Wilson", she said, as they walked round the deck, "to get me out of that horrid money difficulty. But I'm very glad your generosity isn't going to cost you anything."

Craggs could only reply, with truth, that he knew it would have been a pleasure to both of them to be of any use.

"And how very clever of you to exchange the notes! Do tell me how you managed it?"

"It really was quite simple," said the archdeacon. "I'd seen Michalis put the money in the pocket of his shooting jacket, and when I saw him come out without it, I thought there was a good chance he'd left it there. So I nipped in and made the exchange. There was only that one nasty moment: he might have turned up while I was in his cave—otherwise it was quite easy. No conjuring tricks required!"

"All the same, I think it was very clever," said Phyllis, "and that scene this morning; it was quite priceless! I hope it'll keep her in order for the rest of the cruise, and then, thank goodness! I shall part from her for good. But even she hasn't been able to spoil the trip: I shall never forget it!"

The conversation inevitably drifted into a discussion of Miss Hillcroft's plans for the future: it appeared that they were regrettably indefinite. The moon was now shining on the sea, and such conditions are notoriously favourable to the growth of the tender passion. Few of our readers, and none of the female sex (if we are so fortunate as to secure any) will be surprised to learn that, before they left the deck, what is called "an understanding" had been reached between the two parties, and that Miss Hillcroft's future plans had acquired a definiteness hitherto unknown.

Epilogue

"This is a gift very grateful."
—SHAKESPEARE

From *The Times* of Sept. 15:
"CRAGGS-HILLCROFT. On Sept. 14 at Hillcroft St. Mary's, by the Ven. the Archdeacon of Garminster, the Ven. John Craggs, Archdeacon of Thorp, to Phyllis Hillcroft, elder daughter of Frederick Hillcroft and Mrs. Hillcroft of Hillcroft Manor."

Among the wedding presents (which were both numerous and beautiful) figured a plated toast-rack of unpretending design from Lady Mary Culham, a cheque of unexpected magnitude from Mrs. Burslem, and a silver tray sent with the best wishes of the captain and officers of the *Lucretia*.

But there was one which requires somewhat more explanation. On the day before the wedding, the Archdeacon received a small parcel accompanied by a letter which read as follows:

My dear Craggs,

That was really very clever of you! I simply can't think how you managed to let them know where you were: I thought I'd read your letter carefully, but that only shows one can't be too careful. The taking of the notes, too—that was ingenious, though of course on a lower plane.

You will be glad to hear that those good causes of mine (in which I know you only half believe!) did even better than I expected out of the jewels, which sold extremely well.

I was delighted to hear of your engagement, and like to think that Mt. Lasion had some small share in bringing you together.

Epilogue

I've had, thanks to you, to leave it for a bit, but there's no dearth, fortunately, of eligible mountains in Greece. Will you please give the enclosed to Miss Hillcroft, with my best wishes? Dmitri and Spiro, who formed a great admiration for her, ask me to send their respectful greetings.

Yours very sincerely,
"MICHALIS".

P.S. If we ever meet at Lords, perhaps you'll tell me how you did it!

"The enclosed" was a beautiful pearl pendant.

"I do call that nice of him!" said Phyllis.

"Yes, he's not at all a bad chap," said the Archdeacon of Thorp. "What a pity we can't go to Mt. Lasion for our honeymoon!"

Lightning Source UK Ltd.
Milton Keynes UK
12 August 2010
158333UK00001B/6/P